"What distinguishes this novel is its depth of characterization, how O'Connor shows readers who the characters are rather than telling them . . . This heartwarming novel also demonstrates that while dogs may be revered as man's best friend, there's no substitute for the human kind."
—*The Horn Book*

"With keen insight into children's thinking and deep empathy for dogs, O'Connor's story is about finding unforeseen friendships in unexpected places."
—*Parents' Choice*

"Barbara O'Connor is back with another unforgettable middle grade novel. Readers are going to fall madly in love with the characters in *Wonderland*."
—*Sharpread*

"An enjoyable read . . . Two friends and a dog, what could be better."
—*BSCkids*

"A comically sweet story about the power of friendship. Dog lovers will especially enjoy the sections written from the greyhound's point of view."
—*The Plain Dealer*

BARBARA O'CONNOR

Wonderland

SQUARE
FISH

FARRAR STRAUS GIROUX
New York

SQUARE
FISH

An imprint of Macmillan Publishing Group, LLC
120 Broadway, New York, NY 10271
mackids.com

Square Fish and the Square Fish logo are trademarks of Macmillan and
are used by Farrar Straus Giroux under license from Macmillan.

Our books may be purchased in bulk for promotional, educational, or business
use. Please contact your local bookseller or the Macmillan Corporate and
Premium Sales Department at (800) 221-7945 ext. 5442 or by email at
MacmillanSpecialMarkets@macmillan.com.

Library of Congress Cataloging-in-Publication Data

Names: O'Connor, Barbara, author.
Title: Wonderland / Barbara O'Connor.
Description: New York : Farrar Straus Giroux, 2018. | Summary: When her
    mother uproots them again to another home and takes a job as a housekeeper,
    ten-year-old Mavis is determined to find a best friend in Landry, Alabama,
    where the summer also holds the promise of friendship and change for a sad
    man, a stray dog, and a timid girl.
Identifiers: LCCN 2018000293 | ISBN 978-1-250-21138-5 (paperback)
    ISBN 978-0-374-31061-5 (ebook)
Subjects: | CYAC: Best friends—Fiction. | Friendship—Fiction. | Moving,
    Household—Fiction. | Dogs—Fiction. | Alabama—Fiction.
Classification: LCC PZ7.O217 Wo 2018 | DDC [Fic]—dc23
LC record available at https://lccn.loc.gov/2018000293

Originally published in the United States by Farrar Straus Giroux
First Square Fish edition, 2019
Book designed by Aimee Fleck
Square Fish logo designed by Filomena Tuosto

5 7 9 10 8 6

AR: 4.9 / LEXILE: 800L

For Mimi and Leslie

Also by Barbara O'Connor

Beethoven in Paradise

Me and Rupert Goody

Moonpie and Ivy

Fame and Glory in Freedom, Georgia

Taking Care of Moses

How to Steal a Dog

Greetings from Nowhere

The Small Adventure of Popeye and Elvis

The Fantastic Secret of Owen Jester

On the Road to Mr. Mineo's

Wish

Wonderland

MAVIS

Mavis Jeeter sat on the bus stop bench beside her mother and whispered goodbye to Hadley, Georgia. She took a deep breath and let out a big, heaving sigh to send a signal to her mother that she was tired of saying goodbye.

"Why can't we stay here?" she asked every time her mother announced that they were moving.

Then her mother would explain how she was sick of Podunk towns and godforsaken places. How she needed a change of scenery. How she had a friend or a cousin or a boyfriend waiting somewhere else.

This time they were leaving Hadley, Georgia, so her mother could work as a housekeeper for a rich family in Landry, Alabama.

Mavis let out another heaving sigh that blew her

tangled hair up off her forehead. Then she leaned forward and squinted down the road.

"When's the bus coming?" she asked for the umpteenth time.

"Soon," her mother said for the umpteenth time.

Sometimes Mavis wished she lived with her father in Tennessee instead of just visiting him every now and then. Her father stayed in one place. But then, he lived with his mother, who disapproved of Mavis.

"That child runs wild," she complained right in front of Mavis. "Not one lick of discipline from that so-called mother of hers," she'd say, as if Mavis were invisible and not sitting on the couch there beside her. "Lets her run wild," she'd mutter, flinging her arms up and shaking her head.

Finally, the bus came roaring up the road, and the next thing Mavis knew, she was watching Hadley, Georgia, disappear outside the window.

"Goodbye, fourth grade," she whispered when the bus rumbled past Hadley Elementary School. "Have a nice summer," she added.

It was only a few weeks ago that kids had hooted and hollered on the last day of school, but now the window shades were drawn in the empty classrooms.

"So long, Bi-Lo," she whispered when they passed the grocery store where her mother had worked for a few months—until she came home one day and announced, "I'm not asking 'Paper or plastic?' ever again."

"Adios, best friend," Mavis whispered as they drove past Candler Road, where her best friend, Dora Radburn, lived. Then she let out another big, heaving sigh. Actually, now that she thought about it, Dora hadn't really been a best friend. She never saved Mavis a seat at lunch, and she had flat-out lied about her birthday party. Maybe if the Jeeters stayed in one place long enough, Mavis could have a *real* best friend.

So as the bus turned onto the interstate, Mavis said one final goodbye to Hadley, Georgia, and decided right then and there that in Landry, Alabama, she would have a real best friend.

ROSE

Sometimes it seemed to Rose Tully that everything about her was wrong. It also seemed as if her mother reminded her of that nearly every minute of every day.

"Don't slouch, Rose," she'd say.

"You can't wear *that*, Rose."

"Stop slurping your soup, Rose."

But even if Rose sat up straight or changed her dress or sipped her soup as daintily as could be, there would still be something wrong.

And so it was that on a fine summer morning in Landry, Alabama, with the sun streaming through the dining room windows overlooking the garden, Rose plucked raisins out of her oatmeal and waited for her mother to tell her what was wrong.

"Stop *doing* that, Rose," her mother said.

Rose plopped a raisin into her mouth and glanced at her father. Sometimes he would say, "Aw, Cora, cut Rose some slack." But today he didn't. Today he gulped down his orange juice in a way that made Mrs. Tully squint, and then he grabbed his briefcase and hurried out the door without so much as a goodbye.

"Hurry up, Rose," Mrs. Tully said. "There's liable to be traffic on the interstate, and I'm not even sure where the bus station is." She took one last sip of coffee and added, "I'm starting to have reservations about this Jeeter woman if she doesn't even have a car."

"But she's bringing her daughter, right?" Rose said.

"Unfortunately, yes," Mrs. Tully said. "I'm not sure this was one of my better ideas."

Rose folded her napkin and placed it neatly next to her plate. She didn't say it out loud, but she was hoping that this Jeeter woman's daughter was nicer than Amanda Simm.

"Wait for me outside," Mrs. Tully snapped. Then she snatched her napkin off the table, gathered plates and bowls and juice glasses with a clatter, and disappeared through the swinging door into the kitchen, leaving a cloud of discontent behind her.

When Rose opened the front door, a wave of thick summer heat drifted in and mingled with the icy air-conditioning in the foyer. The pleasantly mild days of May had given way to the sultry days of early June, the beginning of a sure-to-be stifling Alabama summer.

Rose's house was the biggest one in Magnolia Estates. It had a winding driveway lined with neatly trimmed boxwoods and a doorbell that chimed Beethoven's "Ode to Joy." On each side of the front door sat a concrete lion, its mouth open in a mighty roar. When the Tullys moved there two years ago, Rose had named them Pete and Larry.

Out on the porch, Rose patted Pete and Larry on the tops of their heads and savored the smell of freshly mown grass. Monroe Tucker, the gardener, had already been there this morning, getting an early start like he always did to beat the midday heat. Because the Tullys' yard was so large, Monroe came three days a week, trimming the boxwoods and weeding the gardens and making sure the azaleas were the exact same height, the way Mrs. Tully liked them.

Rose ran to the end of the driveway and looked up the road toward the gatehouse. She wished she could visit Mr. Duffy instead of going to the bus station with her mother. She wished she could take him some blackberries to try to cheer him up. She wished she could show him how good she had gotten at the magic trick he had taught her. But more than anything, she wished Mr. Duffy's little dog, Queenie, hadn't died.

MAVIS

As they pulled into the bus station in Landry, Mavis's mother went over all the rules again.

Never go into the Tullys' house without knocking first.

Remember to say "Yes, ma'am" and "No, ma'am," because rich people like that.

Don't say anything bad about the garage apartment where they would be living, even if it's a dump.

"And whatever you do," she said, jabbing a finger at Mavis, "be nice to that lady's daughter."

"What's her name again?"

"Rose."

"Rose," Mavis whispered to herself. That was a friendly sounding name.

Okay, *this* time she was not going to beat around the bush.

Rose would be her best friend in Landry, Alabama.

Her mother took a tiny mirror out of her purse and checked her reflection, smoothing her hair and blowing herself a kiss. "Pretty good-looking dame, if I do say so myself," she said, winking at Mavis and tossing the mirror back into her purse. "Okay, May May, let's do this."

Then off she went, strutting up the aisle of the bus like a runway model, leaving Mavis to hurry after her.

ROSE

Rose climbed into the front seat of the Tullys' shiny black car and listened to her mother complain about the heat and about the bad haircut that Darlene Tillman had given her and about Mr. Tully, who never put gas in her car. As they made their way through Magnolia Estates, worry hung over Rose like a thundercloud.

First there was the worry about the vacant lot across the street. In the middle of the lot was a small gold sign with magnolia blossoms around the edges and fancy black lettering that read BUILD YOUR DREAM HOME HERE. Rose wished that people would stop building their dream homes in Magnolia Estates. Before long, there would be no more blackberries to eat or wildflowers to pick or trees to climb. In their place would be big brick houses with tidy lawns kept green all summer by invisible sprinklers that came on in the wee hours of the morning.

When they drove past Amanda Simm's house, Rose's cloud of worry began to grow bigger and darker. Her mother and Mrs. Simm were forever trying to get Rose and Amanda to play together again. But Rose and Amanda weren't very fond of each other anymore. They *used* to play together when they were in third grade, but now that they were going into fifth grade, it seemed as if they had nothing in common. Amanda didn't like tap dancing, and Rose didn't like shopping at the mall. Amanda didn't like playing circus with Pete and Larry, the concrete lions, and Rose didn't like sleepovers. But, for Rose, the icing on the cake was the fact that Amanda didn't seem to like Mr. Duffy, the gatekeeper, anymore. She never actually *said* it, but Rose could tell. Amanda had started making faces when Mr. Duffy told stories about raising pigs in Vermont when he was young. She giggled in a not very nice way when he fell asleep in the gatehouse and delivery truck drivers had to honk their horns. And she rolled her eyes when he pretended to take quarters out of their ears. Now Amanda never went up to the gatehouse anymore, which was fine with Rose.

When the Tullys drove past the gatehouse of

Magnolia Estates, Rose's dark cloud of worry drifted down and settled over her like a blanket of sadness. Mr. Duffy had been the gatekeeper ever since the Tullys had moved there two years ago. He kept a log of who was allowed to come into Magnolia Estates and where they were going. A plumber for the Barkleys on Dogwood Lane. The UPS man delivering packages to somebody on Rosewood Circle. Some ladies playing bridge every other Wednesday at Mrs. Larson's on Camellia Drive.

Mr. Duffy had a way of making Rose feel better about things. He comforted her when she didn't want to go to sleepovers in the Magnolia Estates clubhouse. He knew just the right thing to say when she felt anxious about riding the school bus. And he never made her feel bad if she didn't take flower-arranging classes or piano lessons like her mother wanted her to.

Rose visited him nearly every day. She would tell him about school, and he would tell her about the giant catfish that had jumped clean out of his boat and back into the lake. She would show him the tap steps she learned in dancing school, and he would teach her a magic trick involving paper cups and buttons.

And nearly every day, Mr. Duffy's little dog, Queenie, had waited patiently for Rose to drop graham cracker crumbs or popcorn or maybe even to toss her a piece of cheese. She would bark at the Glovers' cat and take treats from the telephone repairman and waddle out to the edge of the road to watch the trucks bringing bricks for somebody's dream home.

But now Queenie was gone, and Mr. Duffy didn't do magic tricks or play checkers anymore. He didn't play the kazoo while Rose sang "Oh My Darling, Clementine." And he didn't say "Look out, catfish, here I come" when it was time to go home to his tiny trailer out by the lake.

So as the Tullys' shiny black car made its way up the interstate toward the bus station, Rose thought and thought and thought about how she could cheer up Mr. Duffy.

MAVIS

Mavis hopped on one foot around the bus station, careful to only land on the black squares of the linoleum floor. If she touched a white square, something bad would happen, like maybe she would lose that heart-shaped good-luck rock she had found in their yard in Georgia, or her dad would change his mind about letting her spend Christmas with him in Tennessee.

"You're giving me a headache," her mother said, closing her eyes and massaging her temples.

"When are they getting here?" Mavis asked, hopping over to the window and peering into the empty parking lot.

Her mother rummaged through her purse and pulled out another pack of gum. She had been chewing gum constantly for the last three days. Mavis knew that what she really wanted was a cigarette, but Mrs. Tully had been very clear about the no-smoking rule.

"Highfalutin people don't care if they're late," her mother said.

"How do you know they're highfalutin?" Mavis asked.

Her mother popped a piece of gum into her mouth and said, "Believe me, I know."

"So why do you want to work for highfalutin people?" Mavis said.

"In case you haven't noticed, Miss May May," her mother said, "it takes money to get anywhere in this world. If highfalutin people want to give me money for the pleasure of changing their sheets when they're not even dirty or serving them sliced cantaloupe on china plates, I'm willing to give it a shot."

Uh-oh. Give it a shot? That had a *temporary* ring to it. Mavis had hoped that maybe this move to Alabama would be permanent. Or at least till she finished fifth grade. So Mavis decided that she would have to make Rose her best friend right away.

Just then, a shiny black car turned into the parking lot. A lady and a girl got out and walked toward the station.

The lady wore a flowered skirt and a ruffly white blouse. Tucked under her arm was a tiny purse the same color as her shoes.

Mavis was surprised to see that the girl wore a skirt, too. Why would a kid wear a skirt in the summertime? The girl's mousy brown hair was pulled neatly into a ponytail tied with a purple ribbon. Mavis's mother had said the girl was the same age as she was, but this girl looked younger, short and skinny and practically running to keep up with her mother, who marched across the parking lot toward the door of the bus station.

Mavis's mother quickly took the gum out of her mouth and stuck it under one of the plastic seats in the station. She smoothed her hair and brushed doughnut crumbs off her shorts and reminded Mavis for the gazillionth time to say "Yes, ma'am" and "No, ma'am." Then she set a smile on her face and called out, "Mrs. Tully! Over here!"

Mavis watched that highfalutin woman make her way toward them, and it didn't take a genius to see that she was disappointed. Maybe it was her mother's shorts that might have been a little too short. Maybe it was Mavis's wild tangle of hair that hadn't seen a comb since they'd left Hadley yesterday afternoon. Or maybe it was the smell of greasy food and bus fumes that swirled around the dreary bus station.

But whatever it was, it was clear that Mrs. Tully was struggling to make her mouth smile as her eyes darted from Mavis to her mother to the battered suitcases at their feet.

ROSE

The woman tugged on her shorts and thrust her hand toward Mrs. Tully. "I'm Luanne," she said.

Mrs. Tully set her mouth in a hard line and said, "*Mrs. Jeeter* seems more appropriate. I mean, under the circumstances."

"Well, okay, but it's *Miss* Jeeter."

Rose stood behind her mother, feeling shy, as usual. She wasn't very good at meeting new people, especially in front of her mother, who would always give her a nudge and tell her what to say. "For heaven's sake, Rose," she'd scold, "introduce yourself."

"Well, okay then, Miss Jeeter," Mrs. Tully said. "I hope your bus ride wasn't too bad." She gave her hair a pat and added, "I imagine those buses can be pretty horrid."

Miss Jeeter shrugged and said, "It's not like I haven't put in my time on a bus. But avoid the seats in the back, where the bathrooms are, if you know what I mean." She winked at Mrs. Tully, who cleared her throat and shifted her purse from one arm to the other.

And then, much to Rose's surprise, Miss Jeeter's wild-haired daughter came hopping over on one foot and said, "I'm Mavis. You be my best friend, okay?"

Rose looked around the bus station to see if there were any other kids there. Was this girl talking to *her*? Best friend? In all her ten years, she had never really had a best friend. Well, maybe one. Ida Scoggins. She had lived next door to the Tullys in Magnolia Estates when they first moved there. She had taught Rose how to make origami frogs and let Rose walk her dog named Frenchie, who wore a sweater and once bit Monroe Tucker, the gardener. She always made Rose laugh by doing the hula in the sprinkler or putting chopsticks in her nose. Then one day Ida had painted Rose's fingernails bright red. The name of the color was Va-Va-Voom, and Rose had loved it. But Mrs. Tully called Ida's mother, and after that, Ida didn't seem to want to play much anymore. And then the Scoggins moved to North Carolina, and that was the end of that.

And now it seemed like the other girls in Magnolia Estates only wanted to shop at the mall with Amanda Simm and weren't interested in playing cards with Mr. Duffy. So when Mavis Jeeter said, "You be my best friend, okay?" Rose felt a little wave of happiness work its way from her toes to the top of her head.

"Okay," she said, feeling her cheeks burn.

"Shall we go?" Mrs. Tully motioned toward the Jeeters' beat-up bags before heading for the door to the parking lot.

Miss Jeeter snatched up a duct-taped suitcase and followed her.

"Help me carry this," Mavis said to Rose, picking up one end of an overstuffed duffel bag.

Rose took the other end, and the girls hurried out to the parking lot.

Rose could hardly believe how good this day had turned out. Just yesterday she had spent the afternoon sitting alone on the porch between Pete and Larry, and now here she was carrying a duffel bag with her new best friend.

MAVIS

While Mavis's mother chattered away in the front seat, telling Mrs. Tully about taking French cooking lessons at the YWCA with her cousin Elmira, who was in a Toyota commercial, Mavis told Rose about all the places they'd lived.

"And one time, we lived in a condo in Atlanta that had a Jacuzzi in the bathroom," she said. "But the landlord got mad 'cause we had a dog."

"What'd you do?" Rose asked.

"Gave the dog to my uncle Jerry."

"Oh."

"Once we lived with this crazy lady named Trixie who saved everything," Mavis said. "Like used paper cups and empty soup cans."

"Really?"

"And one time we lived over a Chinese restaurant, and I got free fortune cookies."

Rose's eyes grew wide. "How many places have you lived?"

"A bunch. But I might go live with my dad someday."

"Where does he live?"

"In Tennessee with his mother." She leaned toward Rose and added, "She's kind of mean, so that's a problem."

"Your grandmother?"

Mavis nodded. "I was supposed to stay there all summer last year, but she made me leave early."

Mavis was surprised to see Rose suddenly look a little sad. It was their very first day together as best friends, and already Rose felt bad about Mavis's mean grandmother. That was a good sign.

As the Tullys' car made its way up the interstate, Mavis ran her hand over the soft leather seats. Then she took off her flip-flops and wiggled her toes in the thick black carpet under her feet. There wasn't a speck of dust or a single crumb on that carpet. When Mavis's mother drove her boyfriend Mickey's car, the floor was always littered with moldy french fries and dirty napkins and gravel from the driveway. But then, when the transmission had gone, her mother had left the car on the side of the road, which made Mickey mad as all get-out. He and her mother had hollered at each other, and two days later Mavis was packing her duffel bag again.

Before long, Mrs. Tully turned off the interstate and zigged and zagged until they reached a wrought-iron gate across the road and a sign that read MAGNOLIA ESTATES.

"This is where you live?" Mavis asked Rose.

Rose nodded.

"Why is there a gate?"

But Rose didn't answer. She was waving to a gray-haired, whiskery-faced man in a small brick gatehouse.

"Who's that?" Mavis asked.

"Mr. Duffy." Rose kept waving out the back window of the car as they drove into Magnolia Estates. "He's really sad," she said.

"How come?"

"His dog died."

Rose looked down at her hands in her lap, and Mavis thought she was going to cry.

"What happened?"

Rose looked up. "What do you mean?"

"What happened to his dog?"

"She just got old." Rose let out a little sigh. "Mr. Duffy used to do magic tricks and play his kazoo and stuff. But he doesn't anymore. He never even wants to play checkers."

"Then we'll cheer him up," Mavis said.

"I've been trying."

"What've you tried?"

"Well, I took him some blackberries. And I showed him a new card trick from a magic book I got at school."

Mavis let out a little *pfft*. "You gotta do more than *that*."

"Like what?"

"I'll think of something." Mavis poked Rose's arm and added, "Trust me."

ROSE

Rose and Mavis tagged along while Mrs. Tully showed Miss Jeeter around the house. Rose couldn't help but notice her mother's face each time Miss Jeeter piped in with a comment.

"Dang!" Miss Jeeter said, motioning at silver trays and pitchers and bowls on the pantry shelf. "That's a lot of polishing!"

"You gotta be a rocket scientist to figure that thing out," she said, pointing to the knobs on the gas stove. "But I'll get it," she added quickly.

"Check this out, May May!" She tugged on Mavis's arm. "A laundry chute!"

Rose could tell her mother was getting irked. That was a word she used often at the supper table when she told Rose's father about her day. Someone had almost always irked her.

So Rose asked Mavis if she'd like to go upstairs to her bedroom.

"Sure!" Mavis said.

Rose led Mavis up the winding staircase and down the hall to her room.

"Holy cannoli!" Mavis said as she flopped onto Rose's bed. "A canopy!"

Then she jumped up and ran over to Rose's closet and began to count the dresses, ending with a loud "Seventeen!" and making bug eyes at Rose.

Mavis darted around the room, touching and counting and thwacking her forehead and saying "holy cannoli" a few more times.

When the sound of Miss Jeeter's voice echoed up the staircase from the dining room and twined around with Mavis's voice there in her bedroom, Rose suddenly realized how quiet their house usually was.

It was especially quiet since her sister, Grace, had gone away to college last fall. Sometimes Rose went into Grace's room to touch her things. The white leather jewelry box with gold initials. The ceramic cat with a ribbon for a collar. The flower vase filled with bird feathers.

It was boring at home without Grace, who was always so surprising. She would up and do the most unexpected things, like buy a ratty old motorbike with her babysitting money or roller-skate in the foyer when their mother's garden club was there. Once she had brought a boy named Rocky home for supper without even asking. She just sat right down at the dining room table and said, "Pass the chicken," without even introducing him. He had talked about deer hunting the whole time and given Mrs. Tully a headache.

Before Grace left for college, she'd given Rose the shiny silver dollar she had found on the beach in Mobile one summer. Was there anyone else in the whole world who had found a silver dollar on the beach? Rose didn't think so.

Grace had put the coin in Rose's palm and closed her fingers over it. "Hold down the fort, Rosie," she had said.

When Grace finally came home to visit at Thanksgiving, she had a hummingbird tattoo on her wrist. Rose thought it was beautiful, but her parents didn't. Grace had hurried back to school in a huff, and now she was spending the summer with her roommate's family on a lake in Maine. Rose was trying to hold down the fort, but it sure was hard without Grace.

"So," Mavis said as she inspected Rose's books on the shelf under the window seat, "since we're best friends, we should have a club."

A club?

Rose had never been in a club before, unless you counted the Junior Garden Club her mother had made her join in third grade. But she hadn't liked that club very much and had disappointed her mother when she dropped out after only a few meetings.

"What kind of club?" she asked.

"You know, like a Best Friends Club," Mavis said as she examined Rose's collection of china horses.

"Oh. Okay." Rose wasn't too sure about letting Mavis handle her china horses, but she didn't say anything. Instead she said, "What will we do in the club?"

Mavis moved on to Rose's stuffed animals in the doll bed. Rose hoped Mavis didn't think the doll bed was too babyish like Amanda did. She was relieved when Mavis just ran her hand over each stuffed animal and then gave the doll bed a little pat of approval.

"Well, for starters," Mavis said, "we can think of ways to cheer up Mr. Duffy."

"Okay."

Rose felt a tingle of excitement.

Suddenly things seemed a lot better in Magnolia Estates.

MAVIS

"Well, it's not exactly the Ritz-Carlton," Mavis's mother said, dropping the suitcase onto the bed. She opened bureau drawers and peered into the closet and inspected the cupboards in the kitchenette. "Heck," she said, "it's barely even the Motel 6."

Mavis liked the little apartment over the Tullys' garage. Well, it wasn't really an apartment. More like just a room. But it had everything they needed. Beds and bureaus. A stove and a refrigerator. A closet and a bathroom. There were small ruffled pillows on the beds that matched the flowered curtains and the armchair in the corner. All the dishes in the kitchen cupboard matched, even the cereal bowls and the coffee mugs.

And it was way better than her dad's house in

Tennessee, where she had to sleep on the couch when she visited, and it smelled like mothballs and too many cats.

Mavis had a good feeling about this place. She'd only been here one day, and she already had a best friend and her own bureau.

But Mavis's mother strolled around the room, examining things and grumbling.

"Some people get mansions, and the rest of us get one little ole room."

She turned on the tiny television on top of one of the bureaus. A soap opera came on. Two women were arguing about a man named Todd.

"At least the TV works," her mother said. "But a toaster oven would've been nice." She turned the television off and dropped onto the bed. "This might've been a mistake."

Here we go again, Mavis thought.

"Doesn't seem like a mistake to me," she said. "We don't have to pay one penny for this room. And the Tullys' house is like a castle. It sure beats working at the Early Bird."

The Early Bird Café was the last place her mother had worked in Hadley, Georgia. She used to come home every afternoon and tell Mavis that those hillbillies who ate there didn't even know how to *spell* the word *tip*, much less leave one. Then she had gotten into an argument with some lady who complained about her fried eggs, so Mr. Harding, who owned the café, told her to leave.

"I couldn't get out of that dump fast enough," she had told Mavis when she got home.

Mavis could have made a list of all the good things about her mother working for the Tullys. Like the central air-conditioning and the shiny marble foyer. That huge vase of real flowers on the dining room table. The French doors that opened out to the patio, where the gardener watered the potted ferns on the rock wall along the walkway that led down to the biggest, greenest lawn Mavis had ever seen.

But instead, Mavis said, "Rose is my new best friend."

Her mother rolled her eyes and flopped back on the bed.

Mavis went down the steps and into the garage to look around. She had never seen such a tidy garage. On shelves along one wall were large plastic trunks labeled with things like OUTDOOR CHRISTMAS LIGHTS and COVERS FOR ADIRONDACK CHAIRS. On another wall, shovels and rakes and hoes hung on pegs. In one corner was a pink bicycle with silver tassels on the handlebars, a red wagon with wooden sides, and a skateboard. Mavis loved riding skateboards. She used to have one at her father's house in Tennessee. But then her grandmother ran over it with her car and wouldn't buy her another one.

"When you leave nice things in the driveway, you don't deserve to have nice things," she had said in that mean way of hers.

Just then Rose appeared in the doorway. "Do you want to meet Mr. Duffy?" she asked.

"Sure! Can I use this skateboard?"

"Um, I guess."

"Is it yours?"

Rose nodded. "My uncle AJ gave it to me, but I don't really know how to use it and my mom doesn't want me to, anyway."

"Why not?"

"Too dangerous," Rose said. "She won't even let me go barefoot. That's how you get ringworm."

"I go barefoot all the time. Do I look like I've got ringworm?" She held her arms out for Rose to examine.

Rose shook her head.

Mavis grabbed the skateboard and headed toward

35

the door of the garage. "Well," she said, "if I were you, I'd do it anyway."

"Do what?"

"Go barefoot."

"You would?"

"Sure," Mavis said. "It's summer. You're supposed to go barefoot in the summer."

But Rose just looked down at her sandals.

Then off they went to the gatehouse, Mavis riding the skateboard and Rose running along behind, her sandals slapping on the asphalt road.

HENRY

Somewhere in the woods, a very skinny dog lay curled up tightly on a bed of rotting leaves. The dog was white with a large brown spot in the shape of Texas on his side. His nose was long and thin. His legs were long and thin. His tail was long and thin.

Suddenly he was awakened by a noise.

Slapping noises and the whirring of wheels on the asphalt road.

The skinny white dog stood up and cocked his head. Maybe he should follow the noises instead of hiding in the woods.

But then again, maybe not.

Maybe he should stay right here.

So he sat in the leaves and let out a tiny whine as the slapping and whirring grew fainter and fainter.

ROSE

"This is Mavis," Rose said to Mr. Duffy. "Her mother is working for us now, and they moved into the apartment over our garage."

Before Queenie died, Mr. Duffy would've said something like, "Well, hot dang! We should have a cupcake party." Or, "Glory day, ain't that nice?"

But today he smiled a half-hearted smile and shuffled over to his beat-up desk chair, where he spent the day opening the gate for cars and trucks to drive in and out of Magnolia Estates. He dropped into the chair with a sigh. "That's nice," he said.

"Why is there a gate?" Mavis asked, peering out of the little sliding window over Mr. Duffy's desk.

"To keep the riffraff out," he said, giving Rose a wink.

Rose felt her cheeks grow hot. *Riffraff* was the word her mother used to describe the people who weren't allowed to come into Magnolia Estates.

"Rose said you do magic tricks." Mavis pushed at her tangle of curls. "Wanna see one I can do?"

Mr. Duffy nodded, but Rose could tell he didn't care that much about Mavis's magic trick.

"I used to be really good at it, but I haven't practiced in a while," Mavis said, pulling a penny out of her pocket. She closed her fingers over it and then waved her other hand dramatically and said, "Abracadabra sis boom bah!"

Then she opened her hand, and there in the middle of her palm was the penny. Mavis said, "Dang!" and stamped her foot, making the penny fall out of her hand. It bounced across the linoleum floor and settled right in the middle of Queenie's bed beside Mr. Duffy's chair. The fluffy round dog bed with QUEENIE embroidered in blue.

Rose and Mavis and Mr. Duffy stared at the penny.

Rose could practically see Mr. Duffy's sadness hovering over him and then coming to life right there in the gatehouse. It flopped over the little television on the desk and snaked in and out of the coffee cups and newspapers and wrinkled paperback novels with cowboys on the covers. It climbed over the droopy begonia on the windowsill and wrapped around the coffee maker on the file cabinet. And just when Rose thought that sadness would gobble them up like Godzilla, she hurried over and scooped the penny off Queenie's bed. Then she stood there, breathing in the thick, awkward silence until Mavis started jibber-jabbering about how she needed to practice that trick and how she did it perfectly in a school talent show last year.

Rose tried to make her eyes stare down at her sandals, but instead they looked over at Queenie's water bowl in the corner.

Then they looked at Queenie's leash hanging from a nail by the door.

Then they glanced down under the desk at Queenie's dirty stuffed monkey with the squeaker torn out.

Don't look at Mr. Duffy, Rose told herself.

But she did.

Mr. Duffy's shoulders drooped, and his weathered hands lay limply in his lap. His thin gray hair stuck out every which way under his cap.

Was this sad old man the same one who used to dance around the gatehouse whistling his made-up song, "The Boogie-Woogie Whistle Dance"?

If Rose could do any magic trick in the world, she would bring Queenie back.

She would say, "Abracadabra sis boom bah," and there Queenie would be, curled up in the middle of her bed with her chin resting on her toy monkey. Then she would sit out in the shade with Rose and Mr. Duffy and wait for them to give her a bite of bologna. She would stick her head out the window of Mr. Duffy's rusty old truck, her ears flapping in the breeze. She would chase squirrels gathering acorns beside the gatehouse and wag her tail as she watched the kids at the school bus stop.

And she would not be old.

But, of course, Rose couldn't bring Queenie back, and Mr. Duffy was as sad as a person could be.

MAVIS

Mavis had been told about a gazillion times that she must not go inside the Tullys' house unless she was invited.

"Just because I'm in there making potato salad to put in a sterling silver bowl doesn't mean you have a free admission ticket," her mother said. Then she mumbled something about crystal goblets she had to wash by hand and linen napkins she had to iron and then added, "Well, *la-di-da* is what I think about that."

She examined herself in the mirror on the closet door, patting her hair and then tying the apron Mrs. Tully had given her around her waist.

"So," she said, turning to Mavis, "please don't do anything to make that woman any more irritable than she already is. We've only been here two days, and clearly the honeymoon is over."

Mavis shrugged and headed outside, where Rose was waiting at the bottom of the apartment steps.

"Where should we go?" Mavis asked. They were having their first club meeting today to talk about how to cheer up Mr. Duffy.

"I know a good spot," Rose said.

Mavis followed her through the hydrangea garden, up the flagstone path along the side of the house, down the winding driveway, and across the street to a vacant lot.

BUILD YOUR DREAM HOME HERE read the sign in the middle of the lot. Beyond that, at the edge of the woods, a large pine tree had fallen. Rose sat on the tree trunk and said, "Is this a good place for a club meeting?"

Mavis looked around. Clumps of blackberry bushes and wildflowers were peppered among the weeds and large patches of dry red dirt. Not the best place for a club meeting, but maybe she could find something better later.

"I guess so," she said.

Then she sat on the log next to Rose and said, "I'll be president and you be vice president."

Rose nodded.

Then they talked about things they could do for Mr. Duffy.

Decorate the gatehouse with crepe-paper streamers.

Make cupcakes with sprinkles.

Twirl batons.

"What're y'all doing?"

Mavis looked up to see a girl with hair the color of cantaloupe skipping toward them.

"Nothing," Rose said, crossing her arms and turning red in the face.

"Who are you?" Mavis asked the girl.

"Amanda Simm." The girl tossed her cantaloupe hair over her shoulder and repeated, "What're y'all doing?"

"Nothing," Rose said again.

"Having a club meeting," Mavis said.

"What kind of club?"

"A Best Friends Club. Want to join?"

Then she felt the sharp jab of Rose's elbow in her side.

Amanda's eyebrows arched up. "Do you live in Magnolia Estates?" she asked, plopping down on the tree trunk next to Mavis. Her skin was pale and covered with freckles, as if someone had sprinkled cinnamon on her.

Mavis told Amanda about the little apartment over Rose's garage that she had moved into two days ago.

"And y'all are already best friends?"

"Yep," Mavis said. "Right, Rose?"

Rose nodded.

"Wanna join our club?" Mavis asked Amanda again.

Then she felt another sharp jab of Rose's elbow in her side.

"No, thanks," Amanda said.

"Why not?"

Then this freckled girl named Amanda told Mavis about the friends she had. Girls who lived in the big houses in Magnolia Estates and took gymnastics lessons and were on the swim team. She showed Mavis her beaded bracelet she had made at a sleepover the night before and told her about the tennis camp she was going to later in the summer.

"All the girls in Magnolia Estates are going," she said. Then she glanced over at Rose and added, "Well, almost all."

Mavis felt a twinge of envy. She had been so happy to have *one* friend. Imagine having as many as Amanda did. Maybe if her mother would stay in Landry long enough, she could.

"What do you even do in your club, anyway?" Amanda asked.

"Well, right now we're trying to think of ways to cheer up Mr. Duffy," Mavis said. "Right, Rose?"

Amanda rolled her eyes. "Oh, brother," she said. "He's crazy."

Suddenly Rose jumped up, stalked across the vacant lot, and marched up the road toward her house, leaving Mavis staring gape-mouthed after her on the log beside Amanda.

ROSE

Rose was not one to get mad very often.

Especially at her best friend.

Not that she'd ever really had a best friend.

Besides Ida Scoggins.

And she had never gotten mad at Ida Scoggins.

But now she was mad at Mavis for asking Amanda to join their club yesterday. She was also mad at Amanda for saying that mean thing about Mr. Duffy.

Rose's anger made her feel hot and heavy and dark and bad.

Yesterday Mavis had been her best friend, and now she was someone who wanted Amanda Simm to be in their Best Friends Club.

Why would Mavis want *that*?

It was true that Mavis didn't know about Amanda sticking gum in Rose's hair at church one time. *On purpose.* And she didn't know that Amanda had told some kids at school that Rose used to wet the bed. Mavis didn't know that she and Amanda *used* to be friends, but now Amanda and those other girls whispered to one another right in front of her.

But then, maybe Mavis didn't really care about the club as much as Rose had thought she did.

Maybe Mavis would rather go to the mall with Amanda.

Well, that was fine. Rose would stay up here in her bedroom.

She arranged her books in alphabetical order by author.

She cut pictures of dogs out of magazines and glued them into a spiral notebook.

She drew a hummingbird on her wrist with a pen and then tried to wipe it off, leaving a big blue smudge.

Once or twice, she went to the window and pressed her face against the glass to see if Mavis was in the yard. She tried to see the vacant lot across the street, but the roof of the front porch was in the way.

She heard the steady hum of the vacuum cleaner downstairs.

Rose jumped when her mother stepped into her room and said, "For heaven's sake, Rose, what are you doing up here?"

"Nothing."

"Then go find something to do. Miss Jeeter needs to get in here."

"There isn't anything to do," Rose said. The very instant that those words came out of her mouth, Rose wanted to take them back.

Gather them up like butterflies in a net.

But it was too late.

Now her mother was telling her all the things there were to do, starting with playing with Amanda Simm and ending with going up the street to see the new garden made by the Junior Garden Club.

Rose plodded downstairs and out the front door. When she stepped out of the air-conditioned foyer and onto the porch, the Alabama heat felt thick and heavy. She gave Pete and Larry each a pat on the head and made her way slowly to the end of the driveway.

She needed to talk to Mr. Duffy.

But how was she going to get past the vacant lot

where Mavis and Amanda were probably having a Best Friends Club meeting? Or maybe they were doing gymnastics in Amanda's front yard with some other girls from Magnolia Estates.

And even if she made it to the gatehouse without them seeing her, Mr. Duffy might not feel like talking to her. He might not say, "Hey, Rose Petal!" or, "What's shakin', bacon?" He might not give her butterscotch Life Savers or make up another funny story about how he lost the tip of his finger or any of the other things he always did that made her feel better no matter what.

Rose went back to the front porch and sat on the steps between Pete and Larry. She rested her chin on her knees and closed her eyes and let misery snuggle up beside her. She knew what her mother would say if she saw her sitting here.

"Stop moping, Rose," she would say.

But Rose didn't care.

She moped.

And while she moped, a dragonfly flitted among the flowers in the garden beside the screened porch. The neighbor's fat, grumpy cat sauntered across the lawn. And from somewhere in the woods behind the houses across the street came the loud and mournful howl of a dog.

HENRY

Somewhere in the woods, someone reached a freckled arm through a wrought-iron fence.

The dog backed away, his heart racing.

Then that same someone whispered to him.

Soothing words that made his racing heart settle down.

The whisper was calling him Henry, a name the dog had never heard before.

Trying to coax him out of the bushes.

Telling him everything would be okay.

But when that whispering someone reached toward the bushes and tried to touch him, he turned and ran deeper into the woods.

MAVIS

When Rose had jumped off the log and stormed away up the street, not even stopping when Mavis called her name, Amanda had laughed.

She told Mavis that Rose acted like a baby and wouldn't go to sleepovers. She told her that Mr. Duffy couldn't remember anybody's name and fell asleep in the gatehouse, and lots of people in Magnolia Estates were not very happy about that. Then Amanda had disappeared up the side of the road, leaving Mavis sitting alone on the tree trunk.

That night, Mavis sat in the little apartment over the garage feeling sorry for herself while her mother complained about having to wash and iron curtains.

"Who in the world even does that?" her mother said, rummaging through her purse for another piece of gum.

Mavis wanted to tell her mother how bad she was feeling about Rose, but she didn't. Her mother was liable to say something mean about Rose. So she just sat there, feeling sorrier by the minute. She'd only been in Landry for three days, and already her new best friend was mad at her.

The next day, Mavis fixed herself half a peanut butter sandwich and ran down the apartment steps and around front, where Rose was sitting on the porch between those concrete lions.

"Hey," she called to Rose.

Rose stared at the ground and mumbled a very quiet "Hey."

Mavis ran over and sat on the porch next to her. "Want some of my sandwich?" she asked.

Rose looked a little surprised and shrugged.

"What's the matter?" Mavis said. "How come you left the club meeting?"

Rose brushed something invisible off her shorts and shrugged again.

"Because of Amanda, right?" Mavis said.

"Maybe."

Mavis flapped a hand at her. "She can't be in our club."

Rose's head shot up. "She can't?"

"Nope."

"How come?"

"Because she's mean."

Rose perked up. "Really?"

Mavis nodded. "She said mean things about you and Mr. Duffy after you left."

"She did?" Rose's shoulders slumped.

Mavis's mind raced. Maybe she shouldn't have said that.

"Let's go fix some lunch for Mr. Duffy," she said. "Come on."

Then she ran off up the flagstone path along the side of the house, through the hydrangea garden, up the Tullys' back steps, and right on into their kitchen, with Rose running behind her.

When Mavis burst into the kitchen, her mother looked up from the butcher-block island with shiny copper pots hanging above it.

"Mavis!" she said. "What in the world?"

She had been chopping boiled eggs, and now she

began to rant at Mavis about the rules she had already forgotten while she waved the knife around in the air, sending pieces of egg flying in every direction.

"We're going to take lunch up to Mr. Duffy," Mavis said.

"No, ma'am," her mother said. "You are not."

Mavis stomped her foot and was preparing to go on a tirade when Mrs. Tully walked into the kitchen. When she saw Mavis, she said, "Oh, my, well . . ."

"She was just leaving," Miss Jeeter said, glaring at Mavis.

"When will the egg salad be ready?" Mrs. Tully asked. "I have guests coming any minute now." Then she turned to Mavis and said, "Rose needs to have her lunch now."

Then a most surprising thing happened.

Rose lifted her chin and said, "Mavis and I are taking lunch up to Mr. Duffy."

But then she added a quick "Okay?"

Mavis watched in delight as Rose didn't wait for an answer. She scurried around the kitchen grabbing bread and cheese and chips while her mother's face turned red with disapproval.

Mavis's mother went back to chopping egg salad, slamming the knife hard against the butcher block.

Bang

Bang

Bang

Then Rose and Mavis gathered everything into a grocery bag and hurried out the door.

ROSE

When they got to the gatehouse, Mr. Duffy was in his desk chair snoring away. Rose tapped him lightly on the shoulder. His eyes popped open, and he jumped right up out of the chair.

"Jupiter, Mars, and Pluto, Rose!" he said, clutching his heart. "You're gonna scare me right into my grave."

Rose felt her cheeks burn, and she looked down at Mr. Duffy's scuffed-up brown shoes.

"Sorry," she said. Then she held up the grocery bag. "We figured we could have lunch together. Maybe outside."

Mr. Duffy glanced toward the gatehouse door, where a light summer breeze rustled the leaves of a mimosa tree. Then he sank back into the desk chair. "Well, that's darn nice of y'all," he said. "But I better stay in here. I got myself into some hot water the other day when I stepped outside for one gol-dern minute and didn't hear Mrs. Larson's sister buzzing away on that dang buzzer." He took his cap off and rubbed a hand over the top of his bald head. "Besides," he added, "I don't have much of an appetite these days."

Rose's heart sank. Mr. Duffy *always* had an appetite. She had seen him eat a whole jar of bread-and-butter pickles followed by a meat loaf sandwich and banana pudding and then *still* eat the leftover hushpuppies she had brought him. When her mother had ladies over for lunch, Rose often gathered cucumber sandwiches and little tea cakes with sugary violets on top when her mother wasn't looking. Then she would laugh and laugh when Mr. Duffy pretended he was Reynolds J. Snootbottom III, Mayor of the World, popping them into his mouth one by one and holding his pinkie in the air when he drank tea from an invisible cup.

"Then we'll just eat ours in here," Mavis said, opening the grocery bag. But as she was about to reach inside, she suddenly pointed at some fishing gear propped in the corner of the gatehouse and said, "Hey, Mr. Duffy, you going fishing?"

Rose was surprised when she saw the fishing gear. Mr. Duffy lived in a trailer beside a lake on the outskirts of town. Nearly every day, he and Queenie had gone fishing. He almost never caught anything, but he always seemed to enjoy it.

Why was his fishing gear *here*?

Mr. Duffy looked sadly at the poles and tackle box and said, "Naw. I'm lending those to Fergus Mason for a while. He's coming to pick 'em up when he gets off work."

That meant Mr. Duffy wasn't fishing.

Definitely not a good sign.

Rose thought and thought. What was something he might like to do? Suddenly she remembered a game they used to play on rainy days.

"Wanna play the bottle cap game?" she said, hurrying to the shelf over the desk and taking down a shoe box full of bottle caps.

Mr. Duffy had painted a circle on the floor on one side of the gatehouse and taught her how to play a game tossing bottle caps into the circle from the other side of the room. They had played about a million times, and Mr. Duffy had made a trophy out of tin cans and duct tape and told her she was the champion, even though she wasn't very good at it.

"You teach Mavis how to play," Mr. Duffy said. "I'll watch."

Rose didn't like that idea much, but she explained the game to Mavis, who dashed over to get the bottle caps and began tossing them toward the circle.

"I'll be good at this game," she said.

Sure enough, nearly every bottle cap landed inside the circle.

"Wanna keep score?" Rose asked Mr. Duffy.

But he shook his head and said, "Naw."

So Rose and Mavis played while he stared forlornly out the window, looking like he was a million miles away.

Every once in a while, a car needed to be let in. Mr. Duffy checked his clipboard to see if it was okay for him to open the gate. If the residents of Magnolia Estates were expecting visitors, they called Mr. Duffy and had him put the visitors' names on a list on his clipboard.

Just about the time that Rose and Mavis were getting tired of playing the bottle cap game, a big fancy car with three ladies inside pulled up to the gatehouse. The lady driving rolled down her window and said, "Inez Latham and party to see Charlotte Prescott."

Mr. Duffy put on his reading glasses and squinted down at the clipboard. "Sorry," he said. "Not on the list."

And then a big hullabaloo started. The lady got mad, and Mr. Duffy phoned Charlotte Prescott, and the ladies in the car were saying how ridiculous this was and did they look like burglars.

Rose could hear Mrs. Prescott right through the telephone from clear on the other side of the gatehouse.

"I *did* give you those names!"

"I *told* you about the bridal shower!"

"For heaven's *sake*, Mr. Duffy!"

All the while, Mr. Duffy nodded and said "Yes, ma'am" and "No, ma'am" and "Sorry, ma'am." And then he opened the gate, and, after one last mumble of "Outrageous," Inez Latham drove into Magnolia Estates.

Mr. Duffy shook his head. "I'm losing my mojo, y'all," he said.

"What's mojo?" Rose asked.

"It means, like, your charm, right, Mr. Duffy?" Mavis piped in. "My mom used to use it to get guys to move furniture and stuff. 'I'm using my mojo, May May,' she says."

Mr. Duffy chuckled, and Rose's heart lifted a little.

That was a start, wasn't it?

A chuckle?

But then everything changed when Mavis snapped her fingers and said, "I know what you need! You need to get yourself another dog!"

MAVIS

Rose turned white as a ghost, and her eyes grew wide.

Mr. Duffy's face turned as gray as his hair, and he slumped farther down in the chair until it seemed like he might slide right out of it and onto the floor.

Mavis looked from Rose to Mr. Duffy and back to Rose again.

"What?" she said.

Silence.

Rose's chin began to quiver.

"What's the matter?" Mavis asked.

"No more dogs for me," Mr. Duffy said.

"How come?"

"Too old."

"Too old?" Mavis looked at Rose, who shook her head the tiniest bit, as if sending a signal.

"Too old," Mr. Duffy repeated.

"That's crazy," Mavis said.

Now Rose's head shook faster, and Mavis understood. Rose didn't want her talking to Mr. Duffy about getting a new dog. But Mavis had never been one to take *no* so easily. She hurried over to Mr. Duffy, slumped down and miserable-looking in his chair. Then she put both hands on the arms of the chair and said, "Nobody's ever too old to get a dog."

Mr. Duffy looked up at her from under his bushy eyebrows and said, "I got nothing left in me to give a dog. Look at me. My fingers are all whomper-jawed with arthritis. I practically gotta stick my finger in a light socket every morning to start my heart pumping enough to get out of bed."

He took his baseball cap off and rubbed the top of his head. "Shoot," he said, "even my old gray hair got the heck out of Dodge." He lowered his head so Mavis could see how shiny and bald the top of it was.

"Nope," he said. "Ain't no dog wanna spend a life with an old man crazy as a bullbat and ugly as a mud dauber. And if that ain't enough, I'm so poor I can't afford to pay attention. Nope. No dog for me."

Mavis stomped a foot and said a little louder than she'd meant to, "Well, that's about the sorriest thing I ever heard. There's all kinda dogs out there needing somebody to give 'em a home and love 'em. Dogs don't care about bald heads or money or *any* of that stuff."

Mr. Duffy put his cap back on and picked up his clipboard. "Shoot, before you know it, Saint Peter's name's gonna be on this list, 'cause he's coming to get me. Maybe I can be the keeper of the pearly gates." He winked at Mavis. "Assuming I'm going to heaven, but that might be questionable."

Then he looked up at the ceiling and said, "Keep the coffee warm up there, Edna. I'll be joining you soon."

"Who's Edna?" Mavis asked.

"My wife. So sweet she could give you a toothache. Been gone six years, three months, one week, two days, eight hours and"—he pulled out a pocket watch and squinted at it—"twenty-four minutes."

Then he told Mavis about Edna. The pound cake she made and the dresses she sewed and how she called him Mr. James Earl Duffy when she was mad, which wasn't very often.

"If I had a dollar for every time I met another gal as sweet as Edna, I'd be flat busted broke," he said. "Now she's up there in heaven with my precious old Queenie. The two of them left me down here lonely as a pine tree in a parking lot."

"That's why you need another dog," Mavis said. "Right, Rose?"

But instead of helping her convince Mr. Duffy that he needed another dog, Rose sat there in a pool of pity, looking weepy-eyed and quivery-chinned.

"Well, you two just beat all," Mavis said.

"Aw now, Mavis," Mr. Duffy said. "Don't go gettin' your knickers in a knot. Truth of the matter is, this old sorry life of mine is all vines and no taters, and even my vines aren't looking too good anymore. Ain't a dog on this earth needs a pitiful geezer like me."

Rose sniffed and swiped at her cheeks while Mavis stomped around the gatehouse going on and on about how dogs make things better and they only want a little love and a piece of chicken once in a while.

"A dog could put taters on your vines," she said, trying her best to keep her irritation from making her holler.

At that, Mr. Duffy began to laugh. It started as a

weak smile that turned into a rattly chuckle that turned into a laugh that ended up as a wheezy cough.

He wiped his eyes with a handkerchief, pushed himself up out of his chair, and put his arm around Rose. "What you so down and out about, Rosie?" he said.

Then, much to Mavis's surprise, Rose stood up and began an honest-to-goodness rant.

"I wish you wouldn't talk about Saint Peter and the pearly gates," Rose said in a loud, very un-Rose-like voice. "It scares me when you tell Edna to keep the coffee warm," she went on.

Mr. Duffy kind of stuttered, saying, "Well . . . but . . . I . . ."

Then Rose plopped down into Mr. Duffy's desk chair, crossed her arms, and stared at the floor. "I don't even know what that vines-and-taters thing means, but I wish you wouldn't say it," she muttered.

Mavis had an overwhelming urge to strut right over to Rose and give her a high five. But she stayed still while Mr. Duffy said he was sorry and called her "Rose Petal" and promised he wouldn't tell Edna to keep the coffee warm anymore.

And then a funny thing happened. The irritation that Mavis had felt earlier went marching out the door, and jealousy came slithering in, like a snake in the grass. It wrapped itself around her heart and gave it a squeeze when she saw what good friends Rose and Mr. Duffy were and how much they cared about each other's feelings.

But, Mavis being Mavis, she pushed that jealousy aside and said, "Y'all wanna play the bottle cap game?"

HENRY

The dog hadn't run far when he stopped to rest among the pine trees.

It felt great to run free, but now his hip was bothering him again.

That hip that had been hurting for quite a while, making him limp sometimes.

His fur was matted with burs, and his stomach was empty.

After a while, he decided to return to the spot where the freckled arm had reached through the wrought-iron fence. Something about the memory of that soothing whisper drew him back.

Now someone was crossing the green lawn on the other side of the fence, heading toward the woods.

The dog crouched down low behind a tangle of wild shrubs.

He stayed very, very still. He put his chin on the ground and breathed in the rich earthiness. He wanted to get closer to the fence, but he didn't dare.

What if this wasn't the person with the soothing whisper?

He could hear footsteps on the grass.

He peered through the bushes.

Someone put something on the ground and pushed it toward him, under a nearby rhododendron, and said, "Here you go, Henry."

That same someone with the freckled arm.

A girl.

Calling him Henry.

His nose twitched.

His mouth watered.

Food.

The girl had placed food right there on the ground near him.

"Goodbye, Henry," the girl whispered.

He heard the soft steps on the lawn get fainter and fainter.

He waited until there was only the sound of a wren

singing in the trees above him, and then he walked slowly over to the rhododendron.

There on the ground was a small plastic bowl filled to the brim with food.

Chopped up hot dogs.

A small piece of waffle.

Part of a boiled egg.

Little orange crackers shaped like fish.

He had never seen food like this.

He gobbled up every bite.

Then he sat by the wrought-iron fence wishing that the freckled girl would come back and call him Henry again.

He was feeling scared and lonely.

If being Henry would bring the girl back to whisper to him and give him food, then he would be Henry.

That night it rained. A soft, quiet summer rain that rinsed the leaves and soaked the moss and weighed down the ferns . . .

. . . and filled the plastic bowl with water for Henry.

ROSE

Rose heard a terrible thing.

She heard her mother on the phone talking to Mrs. Owens, who lived next door. They were talking about Mr. Duffy.

Rose was sure of it.

This is what she heard her mother saying:

"And then Lorraine Reese had to honk her horn three times to even get in!"

"I know!"

"He did?"

"Charlotte's bridal shower? Really?"

"I totally agree."

Rose felt a little sick.

Her mother and Mrs. Owens were on the board of

the homeowners' association for Magnolia Estates. They had complained about Mr. Duffy before, but lately it was getting worse. They said he was sleeping too much and forgetting things, like not calling the sprinkler repair company when he was supposed to.

What if they fired Mr. Duffy?

Rose felt a little sicker.

She didn't wait to hear the end of her mother's conversation. She went outside and sat between Pete and Larry and watched Monroe Tucker spreading perfect circles of dark brown mulch around the dogwood trees in the front yard. That familiar cloud of worry hung over her. The more she thought, the more she worried. And the more she worried, the darker and bigger the cloud became.

It was bad enough that Mr. Duffy was so sad about Queenie. But now it seemed as if his sadness was making him old and forgetful.

And if he was old and forgetful, he wouldn't do a good job as gatekeeper for Magnolia Estates.

And if he didn't do a good job as gatekeeper, he would get fired.

And if he got fired, Rose would miss him more than anything.

She tried to imagine not having Mr. Duffy to visit every day, but she couldn't. So she just sat there on the steps between Pete and Larry, watching Monroe Tucker spread mulch.

Suddenly the whirring of a skateboard interrupted her gloomy thoughts. Mavis was speeding up the driveway toward her.

"Hey," Mavis said, jumping off the skateboard.

"Hey."

"What's the matter?"

"Everything."

"Like what?"

Rose told Mavis about her mother's phone call. "What if he gets fired?" she said.

"He won't."

"How do you know?"

Mavis rode the skateboard around in a circle and said, "I just know. Let's go have a club meeting."

So Rose followed Mavis down the driveway to the vacant lot across the street. They sat on the fallen pine tree, and Rose listened to Mavis explain what she called her "surefire plan."

"First," Mavis said, "we find a dog."

"What for?"

Mavis slapped her forehead and said, "For Mr. Duffy. Duh!"

"But he doesn't want a dog."

"He's just saying that."

"Where would we find a dog?" Rose asked.

"That's easy," Mavis said. "There's dogs all over the place."

Rose was not too sure about Mavis's surefire plan.

"*Then*," Mavis went on, "Mr. Duffy will be so happy with his new dog that he won't be sad and forgetful. And everybody in Magnolia Estates will be happy, too." She brushed the palms of her hands together. "Easy peasy," she said, smiling a very satisfied smile.

Rose wanted to believe that Mavis's surefire plan was a good one.

She really did.

But a little doubt was stirring around inside her.

Then, while she was trying to make the doubt go away, Amanda Simm suddenly appeared out of nowhere and said, "I know where there's a dog."

MAVIS

Mavis wasn't sure whether to feel annoyed at Amanda for eavesdropping on their club meeting or excited to hear that she knew where there was a dog. So, Mavis being Mavis, she decided to feel annoyed first.

"Dang, Amanda!" she said, jumping up from the pine log. "Don't be so nosy. Right, Rose?"

Rose stayed sitting on the log and looked down at her sandals. "Um, right," she said, so timid and soft that Mavis started to feel annoyed at *her*, too.

Amanda flipped her ponytail over her shoulder and said, "Fine. I guess I just won't tell y'all about that dog after all." Then she turned and started stalking away.

"Wait!" Mavis called, running after her.

Amanda stopped. She stood straight and stiff with her arms crossed and glared at Mavis.

"Where's the dog?" Mavis asked.

"Why should I tell *you*?" Amanda said. "Since you think I'm so nosy."

Mavis concentrated very, very hard on not saying something mean to Amanda. She counted to ten in her head, took a deep breath, and said, "I forgot that sometimes being nosy is a *good* thing."

Amanda narrowed her eyes and cocked her head. "What's that supposed to mean?"

"Well, um, it means that maybe being nosy can help someone, and me and Rose know someone who needs help. Right, Rose?"

Rose nodded.

"You're talking about that crazy old Mr. Duffy, aren't you?" Amanda said.

Rose jumped up. "He's not crazy!"

"My mother says he is, and so does everybody else in Magnolia Estates." Amanda flipped her ponytail again. "Even *your* mother," she added.

Rose's face grew red, she stamped her foot, and she *hollered* at Amanda.

"He is *not* crazy, and that's mean. He's sad because Queenie died, and you don't even care!"

While on the one hand Mavis was enjoying Rose's outburst, on the other hand she wanted Amanda to tell her about the dog. So she stepped between the two of them and said, "Why don't we just get Mr. Duffy a dog, and then things might get better?"

Rose kept scowling at Amanda, and Amanda kept glaring at Rose, so Mavis said, "Come on, Amanda. Tell us about the dog."

Amanda finally stopped glaring at Rose and said, "Well, okay."

She went over to the pine log and sat down.

"There's this dog in the woods behind my house," she said. "I can't see him very well because he hides in the bushes. He's white with a big brown spot on his side and has a skinny nose. I named him Henry."

Mavis's shoulders slumped. If the dog hid in the bushes, he must not like people. That didn't sound like a good dog for Mr. Duffy.

"He won't let me touch him," Amanda went on. "I tried to a couple of days ago, but he ran off."

"Then for crying out loud, Amanda," Mavis said,

"if the dang dog ran off, how are we going to find him?"

"He came *back*," Amanda said, looking at Mavis with a satisfied smirk. "I put food out, and he came back and ate it. Then he ran off again. But I bet you anything he's still in the woods."

Mavis let out an exasperated sigh. Then, before she could stop herself, she said, "But if he keeps running off, what good is that, you ding-dong?"

Amanda jumped up from the log like her shorts were on fire and stormed across the vacant lot and up the middle of the road toward her house, hands clenched into fists and stiff arms pumping.

Mavis looked at Rose. "Now what do we do?" she said.

Rose shrugged. "I don't know."

"Maybe I shouldn't have called her a ding-dong."

"Probably not."

"We should look for that dog," Mavis said.

"But Mr. Duffy doesn't want another dog."

"I *told* you, he's just saying that. I bet if we got him one, he'd love it."

Rose shook her head. "I don't know. I don't really

think so. Besides, that doesn't sound like such a great dog."

"Maybe," Mavis said. "But we should at least try."

Rose glanced up the road in the direction of Amanda's house. "I don't know," she said again.

"Come on, Rose, don't be such a party pooper. Let's find that dog." Mavis wiggled her eyebrows up and down and gave Rose a little poke on the arm. "Come on, party pooper. Please?" She poked again. "Pretty please?"

Finally, in a tiny little voice that Mavis could barely hear, Rose said, "Okay."

Mavis gave Rose a big, hearty hug and said, "You're the *best* best friend I've ever had. We'll look for that dog first thing tomorrow."

ROSE

The next morning at breakfast, Rose's mother told her father that Amanda Simm was taking diving lessons every afternoon at the Magnolia Estates swimming pool. Then she added, "Rose ought to be doing something like that."

Rose stared down at her raisin toast and said a little prayer in her head. *Please don't make me take diving lessons with Amanda.*

Her prayer was answered when her father looked irritated, because he was trying to read the newspaper. He jabbed a finger onto the paper to mark his spot and said, "Maybe Rose doesn't want to take diving lessons, Cora."

Rose's heart did a little somersault of gladness. She

spread a blob of strawberry jam onto her toast and tried to be invisible.

"Rose doesn't want to do *anything*," her mother said, pouring another cup of coffee. "Except stay up there with that old man the livelong day," she added. "She's got no business there, and, quite frankly, neither does he. I think he sleeps more than he works."

Then she went on and on about Charlotte Prescott and that bridal shower and those ladies who couldn't get through the gate. After that she made a list of all the problems in Magnolia Estates that could have been avoided if Mr. Duffy had done his job. Problems with the landscape company and a Sears delivery truck and the streetlights that needed to be repaired.

Rose's somersaulting heart began to tumble around inside her chest and then squeeze up tight. Her hands froze, one holding the knife, one holding the toast. She cut her eyes sideways and glanced at her father. Sometimes when her mother went off on a tangent like that, her father would say, "Oh, Cora, don't be so dramatic." Then he would wink at Rose, and she would wink back, like they shared a secret.

But this time he just kept reading the newspaper like he hadn't heard those mean words. Then he gave Rose a kiss on the top of her head and went off to work, and Rose finished her toast with an icy-cold silence hanging in the air.

The silence was broken when Miss Jeeter came in and began gathering Mr. Tully's breakfast dishes.

"Please don't stack them like that," Mrs. Tully said. "Bone china chips very easily."

Rose watched Miss Jeeter lower her head and roll her eyes.

"And remember," Mrs. Tully said. "That china doesn't go in the dishwasher."

Miss Jeeter pressed her lips into a thin, straight line. She put two of the plates back on the table so they wouldn't be stacked and started toward the kitchen door with only one plate and a juice glass.

"For heaven's sake, Miss Jeeter," Mrs. Tully said. "Use a tray. There are several in the pantry."

"Yes, *ma'am*," Miss Jeeter said in a way that Rose knew probably irked her mother.

Sure enough, Mrs. Tully lifted an eyebrow and shot Miss Jeeter a look that zipped and zapped clear across the dining room and made Miss Jeeter toss her hair out of her eyes, lift her chin, and walk through the swinging kitchen door so fast that Rose felt a breeze blow across the table.

Her mother set her cup down, making a little coffee slosh over the side. Rose dragged her fork through the hardened glob of cold grits on her plate. Normally, her mother would have told her to stop doing that and just eat them. But today she gathered her garden gloves and clippers from the basket by the French doors and went out to the garden to cut zinnias to put in the crystal vase in the foyer.

Rose jumped up from the table and hurried outside to look for Mavis. Today they were going to try to find the dog that Amanda had named Henry. Rose still wasn't sure about this idea. First of all, Mr. Duffy didn't *want* another dog. And second of all, she wasn't allowed to go into those woods.

But Mavis had told her to stop worrying so much.

Mavis had said, "Trust me."

And Rose really wanted to trust Mavis.

HENRY

Somewhere in the woods, Henry slept soundly in the shade of a white oak tree. The morning sun was still low in the sky, but the air was already hot and damp.

A red-speckled salamander scampered over the leaf-covered ground nearby, and Henry woke up. He yawned and stretched. His long, thin legs were scratched and matted with dried mud. The brown spot in the shape of Texas on his side was patchy with itchy bald spots.

His hip was throbbing, and his stomach rumbled with hunger. He made his way through the dense woods, weaving around the mountain laurel and sparkleberry bushes until he found the spot where he had left the small plastic bowl near the wrought-iron fence.

The bowl was gone.

Henry peered through the rhododendron bushes at the green lawn with the dogwood trees. He lay on the mossy ground and waited. Before long, he heard someone whistle and call for Henry. He lifted his head and stayed very still.

His heart pounded as he watched the thin, pale arm reach through the fence and push the plastic bowl under the rhododendron beside him.

The arm was sprinkled with freckles.

Then the arm disappeared, leaving the bowl on the ground nearby.

Henry leaped to his feet and gobbled up the pieces of ham and cold spaghetti and saltine crackers from the bowl.

MAVIS

Mavis slapped a hand on Rose's shoulder and said, "Don't worry. I've got good gut feelings. Shoot, one time I told Mama I had a gut feeling there was a black snake in the trunk of her boyfriend's car, and, sure enough, there *was*. So I have this gut feeling that we're going to find that dog in the woods and that he won't belong to anyone and that Mr. Duffy will love him and everything will turn out good."

"I'm not allowed in those woods," Rose said.

Mavis rolled her eyes. "Oh, good grief, Rose," she said. "No one's gonna even know we're there. Besides, that's a dumb rule."

"But what if Amanda's back there?"

Mavis let out a big, heaving sigh and ran a hand

through her hair. "Who cares about Amanda?" she said. "Besides, she won't even see us. We'll be sneaky. I'm *really* good at being sneaky."

"But if she does see us, she'll tell her mama and her mama will tell my mama and—"

"Okay," Mavis said. "If you don't want to come with me, that's fine. I'll go by myself."

So she headed toward the driveway, walking real slow to give Rose time to chase after her. Sure enough, Rose ran up beside her and said, "Wait! How about if we go this afternoon? Amanda has diving lessons at the pool."

"Well . . ." Mavis looked toward the driveway, then back at Rose. "I suppose. Then what are we going to do now?"

"Let's go see Mr. Duffy."

"Okay."

"But don't say anything about another dog, okay?" Rose said.

"Okay."

So the two of them headed off up the road toward the gatehouse.

Mr. Duffy was wearing the same plaid shirt he'd worn yesterday. His baggy pants dragged on the floor as he ambled around the gatehouse, watering the droopy, yellowing begonia.

"I guess I've been neglecting this thing a bit," he said.

Mavis took the clipboard off Mr. Duffy's desk. "Is this today's list of visitors?" she asked.

Mr. Duffy shook his head and frowned at some papers on his desk. "That baby they hired to work the night shift went and mixed up all my stuff." He tossed some papers into a drawer. "Kid's only got one oar in the water, if you ask me."

Mavis nodded at some packages in the corner of the room. "What are those?"

"Some packages that came for the Grahams over on Mimosa Drive when they were on vacation last week," Mr. Duffy said.

"Did you tell them they're here?" Rose asked.

"Of course I did," Mr. Duffy snapped. "Believe me, those biggety folks'd be flinging a hissy fit if I hadn't." He took a sip of coffee from a mug that had GREAT SMOKY MOUNTAINS NATIONAL PARK on the side with a picture of a bear.

"But naturally, I didn't tell them *fast* enough," he said. "Everybody's so all-fired impatient these days. They wanna eat the corn pudding before the corn's even planted."

Mavis pointed to the dog bed beside Mr. Duffy's chair. The fluffy round bed with QUEENIE embroidered in blue. "You ought to give that to the Salvation Army. I bet there's lots of people who could use it for their dog."

Mavis jumped when Rose jabbed her with her elbow.

Hard.

"That's Queenie's bed," Rose said.

Mr. Duffy looked at the bed with sad, watery eyes and scratched his chin.

"I reckon I ought to get rid of that thing," he said. "That do-nothing Jarvis who works the weekend shift keeps grumbling about it."

"Or you could save it for another dog," Mavis said.

Rose widened her eyes at Mavis and shook her head.

Uh-oh. Mavis had gone and done it again.

Sorry, she mouthed silently to Rose.

"I have to go," Rose said and marched out of the gatehouse, her sandals slapping on the linoleum floor.

Then the phone on Mr. Duffy's desk rang, making him jump. Somebody on the other end of the line was hollering and a car behind the appliance repair truck honked and Mavis decided it was time to go home.

* * *

While Mavis sat on her bed and watched TV in the little apartment over the garage, her mother heated leftover macaroni and cheese in the microwave and complained.

"I don't know why they have to eat every meal in that dining room. Would it kill them to eat in the kitchen like normal people do?" she said. "But no. I have to schlep that precious china in and out about a hundred times a day."

Mavis turned the television up a little louder.

"And you'd think maybe they could use a paper napkin once in a while so I wouldn't have to wash and iron those fancy cloth napkins of theirs." She wrote a big *T* in the air with a finger and added, "Monogrammed, of course."

She scooped macaroni and cheese onto a paper plate and brought it to Mavis.

"Tomorrow I'm supposed to make melon balls," she said. "Who in the world has even *heard* of melon balls?"

Then she jerked open the tiny window over the sink and lit a cigarette.

"This might've been a big mistake, May May," she

said after blowing a stream of smoke through the window screen. "Oh, and you should've heard her when I used a dust rag on that ole painting in the library," she went on. "You'd've thought that ugly thing was the *Mona Lisa* or something."

She stubbed her cigarette out in the sink. "Library," she said, rolling her eyes, and then let out a little *pfft*. "I'm telling you, May May, that woman's got her nose so far up in the air she's gonna drown in a rainstorm."

She flopped down on the bed and draped an arm over her eyes. "The best part of the day is taking the garbage out when Monroe Tucker is in the garden," she said. "He's a bit of a looker, don't you think, May?"

But Mavis didn't answer.

She was too busy thinking.

She was thinking about Rose, who was mad at her for mentioning getting another dog to Mr. Duffy when she had promised she wouldn't.

She was thinking about why she was so bad at being a best friend.

And she was thinking about how she was going to find that dog, Henry.

ROSE

Rose couldn't believe that she was mad at Mavis again.

But she had every right to be mad.

Didn't she?

Hadn't Mavis gone and done exactly what Rose had asked her not to do?

It nearly broke Rose's heart thinking about Mr. Duffy's face when Mavis said that about giving Queenie's bed to the Salvation Army.

When she had gotten home, Rose had gone up to Grace's room and sat on the thick pink carpet. She looked around at Grace's gymnastics ribbons taped to the dresser mirror, the dried-up prom corsage on the bookshelf, the teddy bear some boy had given her nestled in the cushions of the rocker by the window. Before long, Rose realized she wasn't mad anymore. Maybe a little sullen and brooding, but not actually mad.

After a while, she went downstairs to the library and called Grace. She used to call her every day, but Grace was always busy doing fun things at that lake in Maine. So now she only called when she really, really needed to talk.

Today, Rose really, really needed to talk.

The phone rang and rang, and Rose was ready to give up when Grace answered in that breathless way of hers, saying, "Rosie!"

Rose told Grace how worried she was about Mr. Duffy. How he seemed so sad and how folks in Magnolia Estates were always complaining about him.

And Grace said the perfect Grace thing.

"Aw, those old biddies complain about everything. Don't worry about it."

Then Rose told her about her new friend, Mavis. How they had a Best Friends Club and how Mavis wanted to find a dog for Mr. Duffy.

"A Best Friends Club?" Grace squealed. "That's great, Rosie! And looking for a dog sounds like fun."

Rose felt a wave of comfort settle over her. Grace had a way of doing that.

She was going to tell Grace about the dog in the woods, but then she heard girls jabbering and laughing in the background, and Grace said she had to go.

After that, Rose went outside and found Mavis, who was drawing with chalk on the apartment steps.

"I'm sorry I got mad," Rose said.

Mavis looked up from her drawing and said, "That's okay." Then she put the chalk down and stood up. "I shouldn't have mentioned a dog to Mr. Duffy again. You asked me not to, but I did anyway." Mavis blushed a little and added, "I'm sorry."

Then Mavis made up a special handshake that involved slapping palms and snapping fingers and bumping fists. They practiced it over and over until they could do it perfectly every time. Then they made a plan to look for the dog in the woods the following afternoon.

That evening at supper, Rose took tiny bites of creamed corn and tried hard not to make a face. Making faces over food she didn't like irked her mother.

Her father was on his third helping of beef Wellington and sipping red wine when her mother launched into a tirade about Mr. Duffy.

"Gerald Berkley said nearly every time he gets to the

gatehouse, the coffee is practically burnt up in the bottom of the pot with the coffee maker *on*."

Mr. Tully glanced at Mrs. Tully.

A most disinterested glance.

Then he sliced a piece of beef Wellington and said, "Who is Gerald Berkley?"

Mrs. Tully crossed her arms.

"I *told* you," she said. "The new night-shift gate-keeper."

Mr. Tully just nodded and said, "Oh."

Mrs. Tully went on. "And Connie Jacobs says that when Mr. Duffy goes out to check on something, he leaves the keys right in the door lock so every criminal in town can go in there and help themselves."

"Help themselves to what, Cora?" Mr. Tully asked.

"I don't know, Robert," her mother said. "Whatever's in there, I suppose."

Mr. Tully lifted his eyebrows, said "Huh," and went back to eating and sipping wine.

"And not only will he not wear that uniform he was given," Mrs. Tully continued, "but he wears the same raggedy clothes day in and day out. It's embarrassing."

"Embarrassing to whom?" Mr. Tully said.

Her mother placed her fork carefully on her plate,

put her hands in her lap, leaned forward, and said, "To everyone, Robert."

She looked at her plate and frowned. "This beef Wellington is way overdone."

Mr. Tully winked at Rose, and she winked back.

The dining room grew quiet. The sound of silver forks on china plates seemed to echo and bounce against the flowered wallpaper and drift up to the crystal chandelier.

When Miss Jeeter came in to clear the table, Rose quickly spread the creamed corn around on her plate so it looked like she had eaten some.

"Do y'all want that sherbert now?" Miss Jeeter asked.

"Sorbet," Mrs. Tully corrected her. "And yes, please," she added.

Rose was certain she heard Miss Jeeter say, "Whatever," as she left through the swinging kitchen door.

That night in bed, Rose thought about that dog, Henry. Would she and Mavis be able to find him? Was he out there in the woods behind Amanda's house right now? And if they found him, would Mr. Duffy want him? And if he wanted him, would he be able to love him as much as he had loved Queenie? And if he loved him that much, would he stop being sad and forgetful?

Rose wished she could be sure about everything, like Mavis was.

But she wasn't.

MAVIS

Mavis rode the skateboard up and down the driveway and waited for Rose to come outside. She wished Rose wasn't such a worrywart.

Worried about going into the woods.

Worried about Amanda Simm tattling.

Worried about Mr. Duffy.

But still, Rose was her best friend. Mavis supposed you had to accept your best friends just the way they are, even if they happen to worry a lot.

When Monroe Tucker started using the weed whacker around the edges of the flower beds, Mavis left the skateboard in the driveway and went around back to peer through the window in the kitchen door. Her mother was in there scrubbing the copper bottom of a pot, something Mavis knew she hated to do.

"I don't get why the bottom of a gol-dern pot has to be shiny and perfect. It's a *pot*, for criminy's sake," her mother had complained just the night before. "Hasn't she ever heard of 'the pot calling the kettle *black*'?"

Mavis opened the door a crack and said, "Where's Rose?"

"How should I know, Mavis? I'm too busy being Cinderella." She slammed the pot onto the kitchen counter and reached for another one.

Mavis pushed the door open, and, before her mother could holler at her, she darted across the kitchen, through the swinging door, over the thick dining room rug, across the shiny marble floor in the foyer, and up the stairs to Rose's room.

"Hey," Mavis said. "Let's go look for Henry."

Rose looked surprised to see Mavis in her bedroom. But she looked even more surprised when Miss Jeeter burst into the room and let out a string of harsh words for Mavis.

What on earth was she thinking, busting into this house like that?

Couldn't she go one day without giving her mother a headache?

How many times had they gone over the rules?

Mavis's answers were short.

"I don't know."

"Yes, ma'am."

"About a hundred."

Then Miss Jeeter stormed off back downstairs. When the stomp, stomp, stomp of her angry footsteps faded and the rattle of pots and pans drifted up from the kitchen, Mavis grinned at Rose.

"Let's go look for Henry," she said.

Rose hesitated but then said, "Um, okay."

So off they went, down the driveway and up the road toward Amanda's house, Rose running along beside Mavis on the skateboard.

When they got closer, Mavis got off the skateboard and said, "Okay, now we have to be stealthy."

Rose didn't answer. She looked around nervously as if Amanda was going to jump out from behind a tree any minute.

"Here's what we do," Mavis said. "We run as fast as we can through Amanda's front yard and then along the fence until we get to the woods. Then we start looking. Easy peasy."

Mavis put the skateboard behind a shrub on the side of the road and motioned for Rose to follow her. Then she took off running across the yard, up the brick walkway that ran beside the garage, along the wrought-iron fence that enclosed the backyard, and into the woods behind the house.

When they were far enough into the woods, Mavis stopped, her hands on her knees, panting.

Rose sat on the ground and dumped dirt out of her sandals and brushed pine needles out of her hair. Then she looked up at Mavis and said, "I don't think I should be here."

"Oh, good grief, Rose, don't be such a scaredy-cat."

"I'm not a scaredy-cat."

Mavis lifted her eyebrows and crossed her arms.

"I'm not," Rose said, not very convincingly.

Mavis shrugged. "If you say so."

Then she started off through the woods, stepping over rotting logs and pushing past tangled vines and overgrown shrubs.

Every now and then, she glanced behind her. Rose was following, looking very unhappy.

Mavis cupped her hands around her mouth and began to call. "Henry! Here, boy! Henry!"

Then, imagine Mavis's surprise when a dog poked its head from behind a cluster of holly bushes.

Mavis stopped.

Rose stopped.

The dog's face was white. His ears were brown. His nose was very long and very thin.

"This is Henry!" Mavis said. "It has to be."

Mavis took a few slow steps toward the bushes, saying, "It's okay, fella. I won't hurt you."

The dog stayed put, watching Mavis with fearful brown eyes, but Mavis could hear his tail wagging.

Swish, swish, swish in the bushes.

"So, what do we do now?" Rose asked.

"I'm going to try and grab him."

"I don't think that's a good idea. He might bite you."

Mavis flapped a hand at Rose. "I'll let him smell me first. That's what you're supposed to do."

Mavis held her hand out toward Henry, who took a slow, careful sniff.

Then she took two quick steps toward the bushes, reaching for him, but he was gone in a blink, jumping over logs and darting around trees before disappearing out of sight, leaving Rose and Mavis alone in the woods.

HENRY

Henry ran and ran and ran until he was sure he was far away from the wrought-iron fence.

He had been so surprised to see two young girls there in the woods, calling that name Henry.

A girl with wild curly hair and a girl with a thin brown ponytail tied with a bow.

When the wild-haired girl had talked to him in that soothing voice, his heart had lifted.

And when she had held her hand for him to sniff, he'd felt comforted.

But when she had lunged toward him, trying to grab him, he'd felt scared.

What if those girls wanted to take him back to Wonderland?

No. He was *not* going back to Wonderland.

So he had run deeper and deeper into the woods.

Now, as he lay on the mossy ground, his stomach growling with hunger, he wished he could go back and see if there was food in the plastic bowl.

But he would wait.

Those two girls might still be there.

ROSE

Rose sat on a stool next to Mr. Duffy's desk and listened to him tell her and Mavis about the kerfuffle yesterday.

That was the word he used.

Kerfuffle.

He told them how Doreen Chapman had marched into the gatehouse and accused him of allowing riffraff into Magnolia Estates. Apparently, the riffraff had been two men in a truck with GREEN THUMB LANDSCAPING on the side.

Green Thumb Landscaping was not authorized to come into Magnolia Estates.

Then the two men had gone door to door to see if anyone needed a landscaper.

Doreen Chapman had said the men looked like reprobates.

"What in the name of Bessie McGee is a reprobate?" Mr. Duffy asked Rose and Mavis. "They looked about as country as a turnip green to me. Just two old country boys trying to make a living."

Mr. Duffy took a box of saltine crackers out of his desk drawer and offered some to Rose and Mavis.

"Then what happened?" Rose asked.

"Aw, she went on and on about this, that, and the other."

Rose wondered what *this, that, and the other* was, but she didn't ask. She didn't want to hear about anything else Mr. Duffy may have done wrong to make Doreen Chapman so mad. It seemed like things were getting worse every day.

Just that morning, Rose's mother had told her father that Mr. Duffy had brought a rickety old fan into the gatehouse, and it had blown a fuse and left burn marks on the wall.

"Now he's going to go and burn the place down," her mother had snapped. "Besides, Gerald Berkley said that if Mr. Duffy would remember to call about the broken air conditioner out there, they wouldn't have needed the fan in the first place."

Rose glanced over at the burn marks on the wall of the gatehouse and frowned.

Mavis made a little stack of saltine crackers on her lap and said, "Doreen Chapman sounds mean."

"Ha!" Mr. Duffy slapped his knee. "Meaner than a wet panther."

Mavis laughed, but Rose didn't.

She hoped Mavis didn't want to go back into the woods to look for Henry again. Why was Mavis so stubborn? She was also pretty bossy. Rose was happy to have a best friend, but she wished Mavis wasn't quite so bossy.

Rose's thoughts were interrupted when Mr. Duffy peered out the gatehouse window and said, "Looks like we're in for some rain."

Sure enough, the sky had turned dark, and there was a low rumble of thunder in the distance.

"Hoo boy!" Mr. Duffy said. "This one's gonna be a gully washer."

Suddenly the rain started, sending waves of steam drifting up from the hot asphalt streets of Magnolia Estates.

So Rose had lucked out. She and Mavis couldn't go back to the woods because it was raining. Instead, they ran to Rose's house and hightailed it up the stairs with Miss Jeeter hollering, "What're y'all doing in here with those muddy shoes? Who do you think has to clean these floors?"

Once inside Rose's room, Mavis collapsed on the bed, laughing.

But Rose didn't laugh. She pointed to the muddy footprints on her fluffy pink rug and said, "My mama's gonna kill me."

Mavis sat up. "It's only dirt," she said. "Dirt comes off, you know."

Then Mavis hurried up the hall and came back with a towel. A thick yellow towel monogrammed with the letter *T*.

She wiped at the rug with the towel, and, much to Rose's relief, the mud came off. Now she only had to worry about the dirty towel.

"Don't be such a worrywart," Mavis said.

Rose frowned down at the dirty towel in her lap. Why *was* she such a worrywart? Why couldn't she be more like Mavis? Mavis didn't care one little bit if her mama yelled at her.

Then, wouldn't you know it, the door opened, and Mrs. Tully looked horrified when she saw the girls in their rain-soaked clothes.

"Mavis, you need to leave," she said. "And Rose, please change your clothes. Mrs. Simm invited us to lunch."

Mavis hopped off the bed and said, "See ya." Then she disappeared through the bedroom door with Mrs. Tully's disapproving looks zapping down the hallway after her.

"Will Amanda be there?" Rose asked.

"I assume so, since her mother asked me to bring you."

And so the good luck that Rose had had when the rain came had run out. She was having lunch with Amanda Simm.

MAVIS

Mavis's mother blew smoke out of the kitchen window and complained.

"And that Mrs. Simm thinks the sun comes up just to hear her crow."

Mavis took a bag of potato chips from the top of the refrigerator and flopped onto the bed. "What does that mean?" she asked.

Her mother tossed her cigarette into the kitchen sink. "Means she's uppity as all get-out is what it means. You should've seen the look on her face when she was telling those bridge ladies about how her husband's the best this and the best that and her daughter's the best this and the best that and *she's* the best this and the best that."

She hopped off the kitchen counter and yanked the refrigerator door open. "I swear, every one of those women are like that. Snooty, snooty, snooty."

She slammed the refrigerator door shut. "I wish we could go *out* to eat once in a while. If I had a car, we could. Maybe I'll take the bus over to the used-car lot this weekend and see what they've got. And maybe if Mrs. Queen of the World Tully would pay me more, I could afford to buy something."

On and on and on she went.

Complaining, complaining, complaining.

Mavis was used to her mother complaining. She complained about Mavis's dad, who never sent money when he was supposed to and was a mama's boy. She complained about jealous boyfriends, nosy schoolteachers, the high cost of cigarettes, and her flabby arms. And she complained about every job she had ever had. But it seemed like this time the complaining had come sooner. They had only been in Landry a couple of weeks.

Mavis took the bag of potato chips out on the little porch at the top of the steps and sat down, looking up at the starry summer sky and thinking about Henry. She and Rose had gone back to the woods behind Amanda's house three more times but hadn't seen him again. Mavis decided that tomorrow they should ask Amanda if Henry was still coming to the fence for food. She knew Rose was scared that her mama would find out she'd been going back in those woods where she wasn't supposed to go. But, dang it, Mavis was determined to carry out her plan of getting a dog for Mr. Duffy.

When Mavis saw Rose walking toward the apartment steps, she got a sinking feeling. Why was she so dressed up? A *sundress*? She didn't look like somebody who was going into the woods to look for a dog.

"Where're you going?" Mavis asked.

Rose looked surprised. "To look for Henry with you."

"But why are you so dressed up?"

Rose looked down at her dress. "I'm not."

"You're gonna go in the woods like *that*?"

Rose blushed. "Um, yeah, I guess."

"Well, I have an idea."

Rose didn't look very interested in hearing Mavis's idea, but Mavis went on. "Let's go ask Amanda if Henry's still coming to get the food back by her fence," she said. "Then we'll at least know for sure that he's still around."

"Oh," Rose said. "Well, um . . ."

"Please?"

Rose hesitated for a minute, but finally said, "Okay."

Then, before Rose could change her mind, Mavis grabbed her hand, and off they ran toward Amanda's house.

ROSE

Rose hated going to Amanda's house.

Amanda always made her feel like a baby, especially when other girls from Magnolia Estates were there. They always talked about things that Rose didn't care about, like soccer and lip gloss.

Rose was also worried about getting her white sandals dirty.

But here she was, running to Amanda's house with Mavis.

When they got to the Simms' house, Mavis leaped right up onto the porch and rang the doorbell while Rose waited on the sidewalk. When Mrs. Simm opened the door, icy cold air floated through the screen door and mingled with the hot summer air on the porch.

"Is Amanda here?" Mavis asked.

Mrs. Simm's face had disapproval written all over it.

Mrs. Simm disapproved of Mavis because Mrs. Simm disapproved of Miss Jeeter.

And Mrs. Simm disapproved of Miss Jeeter because of the things Rose's mother had been telling her.

Just the other day, when Rose and Amanda had sat in silence at the Simms' kitchen table eating banana pudding, their mothers had been in the living room, eating crab salad and talking about Miss Jeeter. They had talked low, but Rose had heard them.

Mostly it was Rose's mother talking.

"And she had no idea what aspic is . . ."

"She put the sheets on the bed without even ironing them . . ."

"And I swear I saw her flirting with Monroe Tucker, strutting up the driveway and flipping her hair. Can you imagine? Monroe Tucker. The *gardener*!"

Mrs. Simm didn't say much. She only said things like "Good heavens" and "Seriously?" and "Good heavens" again.

Now, with Mavis standing on her front porch, Mrs. Simm's eyes traveled from her dirty bare feet to her wild hair, and she raised one eyebrow in a perfect arch. "Yes, she is. Would you like me to give her a message?"

"We need to talk to her," Mavis said.

Mrs. Simm let out a sigh. "Just a minute," she said, closing the door.

Mavis looked back at Rose and said, "Oh brother."

Rose licked a finger and wiped dirt off one of her white sandals. She wished she could go barefoot like Mavis. But Mrs. Simm would see and tell her mother, and her mother would remind her about ringworm. Mavis probably wouldn't care if she got ringworm, but Rose sure would.

After what felt like a long time, Amanda opened the front door. "What do you want?" she said, narrowing her eyes at Mavis.

"Is that dog still coming to your fence to get food?" Mavis asked.

"His name is Henry," Amanda said.

"Then is *Henry* still coming to your fence to get food?"

Rose recognized that tone of voice coming from Mavis. Any minute now, she was liable to call Amanda a ding-dong. Then Amanda would get mad and tell her mother, who would tell Rose's mother that she had come to their house wearing dirty sandals, and Mavis had been barefoot and called Amanda names.

Amanda stepped out on the porch and closed the door behind her. She was wearing a sparkly red headband, and her cantaloupe-colored hair hung perfectly straight down her back. She had once bragged to Rose that she hadn't cut her hair since third grade.

"Don't talk so loud," Amanda said to Mavis.

"Why not?"

"Because my mother told me not to feed Henry anymore or else he'll keep hanging around, and my parents don't want dogs hanging around."

"Why not?"

"Because stray dogs have ticks and fleas and mange and maybe even rabies." Amanda straightened her headband and added, "But yes, Henry ate the cheese I put out there yesterday."

"Are you sure it was Henry and not a raccoon or something?"

"I saw him from the porch," Amanda said. "It was definitely a dog, and I'm pretty sure it was him."

"Great," Mavis said. "Thanks."

Then she hopped down the steps and said, "Come on, Rose."

And just like that, Mavis ran toward the woods behind Amanda's house, leaving Rose standing on the sidewalk.

"She is so rude," Amanda said, and disappeared inside her house.

For a very brief minute, Rose considered going back home.

But she didn't.

She ran off after Mavis, trying her best not to get her sandals dirty.

HENRY

Henry had stayed hidden in the brush when the girl with the freckled arm reached through the fence and put something in the plastic bowl.

He had waited until the girl ran across the green lawn toward the big brick house, then he hurried to see what was in the bowl.

Cheese!

The girl had put little cubes of cheese in the plastic bowl.

Henry had never tasted anything so good.

When he had licked the bowl clean, he noticed that the freckled girl was watching him from the porch of the brick house.

He wished she would come talk to him and pet him and play with him.

But something about the girl told Henry that the family in that house didn't want a dog.

The way the girl whispered.

The way she quickly put food in the plastic bowl and then ran off.

So when the girl stopped to watch him from the porch, Henry had run away.

Now he was sleeping in a pile of damp oak leaves, dreaming about things that dogs dream about.

Playing with dogs.

Chasing rabbits.

Eating cheese.

When Henry woke from his dream, he felt lonely.

He missed his friends at Wonderland.

But he wouldn't go back there.

Because something didn't seem quite right at Wonderland.

MAVIS

Mavis watched Mr. Duffy sort through papers on his desk, then make notes on a clipboard.

"Wanna play cards?" Mavis asked. "Rose and I can teach you how to play I Doubt It. Right, Rose?"

Rose sat on the stool beside the desk and nodded.

Mr. Duffy wiped the back of his neck with a handkerchief. "Naw, you girls play without me," he said.

"Play the kazoo, and me and Rose'll make up a song," Mavis said. "I'm good at making up songs."

Mr. Duffy shook his head and wiped his forehead with the handkerchief. "Aw, I ain't played that thing in so long, I doubt I could wrestle a tune out of it," he said.

Just then the phone on the desk rang. Mr. Duffy answered it.

He said "Yep" and "Nope" and "Yes sirree" and "Beats me" and "You bet your boots" and "Suit yourself."

Mavis noticed that Rose had that worried look of hers, so she piped up and asked, "Who was that?"

Mr. Duffy turned on the little fan on his desk and placed his coffee mug on some papers so they wouldn't blow away.

"That dern fool of a contractor working on that house over on Creekside Drive," he said.

Then he mumbled, "Dumber than a bag of hammers."

"What'd he want?" Mavis asked.

"Wanted to complain," Mr. Duffy said. "Must've figured I hadn't heard enough complaints today."

"What'd he complain about?"

"A bunch of nonsense stuff."

"Like what?" Mavis asked.

"Like the streetlight that's flickering down on the corner and where was the street sweeper that was supposed to clean up that sand in the road and why didn't I let the concrete truck in yesterday and was he going to have to speak to the homeowners' association?"

"Speak to them about what?" Rose asked in a quiet, trembly voice.

Mr. Duffy shuffled across the gatehouse to the coffee maker on the file cabinet in the corner. "That man's all hat and no cattle," he grumbled.

"What does that mean?" Mavis said.

"Means he's all talk."

Then, before she could stop herself, Mavis said, "I bet if you got another dog, people wouldn't complain so much."

Dang it! Why'd she have to go and say that?

Silence settled over the little gatehouse.

Except for that fan.

Rotating back and forth.

Back and forth.

And Mr. Duffy's rattly breathing.

Finally, Mr. Duffy broke the silence.

"You need to pack that idea away, Miss Mavis, 'cause I'm just too tuckered out. There ain't no dog out there that wants an old gizzard-hearted codger like me. Besides that, you could bring a whole passel of dogs in here, and folks'd still be griping. A dog ain't gonna change that."

Mavis wanted to tell him about her plan. That if he was loving a dog again, then he wouldn't be so down in the dumps. He'd be like the Mr. Duffy he'd been before she came to Landry. The Mr. Duffy that Rose had told her about. Doing magic tricks and whistling "The Boogie-Woogie Whistle Dance." And Rose would stop worrying. She wanted to tell Mr. Duffy that Rose was her best friend, and she was pretty sure that's what you do for your best friend—help them to stop worrying.

But Mavis didn't tell Mr. Duffy about her plan.

Still, she was more determined than ever to make it work.

She was going to find Henry.

She was certain that finding Henry would make everything better for Mr. Duffy.

Which would make everything better for Rose.

And then, she, Mavis Jeeter, would be the *best* best friend that anyone could have.

ROSE

Rose sat on Grace's bed, thinking about Mavis's plan to find Henry.

"We'll see if we can find some clues," Mavis had said, "like mashed-down plants where he's slept or maybe even some paw prints on the ground. He has to be close if he's still eating Amanda's food. We'll find him and take him straight to Mr. Duffy. It's the perfect plan."

But Rose didn't think it was the perfect plan.

She glanced up at Grace's bulletin board over her desk. Tacked to it were ticket stubs from a rock concert in Birmingham, an invitation to somebody's high school graduation party, a dried rose, a postcard their cousin had sent from Mexico—and right in the middle was a picture of Grace, sitting on the hood of somebody's car.

She was wearing that silky flowered blouse that Rose loved so much.

Rose wished Grace were here to talk to. Grace would give her good advice about Mavis's plan. Maybe Grace would tell her it was a bad idea. But then again, Grace was a lot like Mavis. She never cared about breaking rules.

Rose went down to the library and dialed Grace's number.

Grace picked up right away and squealed, "Rosie!"

Rose told her about Mavis's plan.

And wouldn't you know, Grace thought it was a great idea.

"Really?" Rose said.

"Sure! Why not?"

Then Grace told Rose she needed to have a little fun once in a while, and there were so many dang rules in that house it might as well be a prison.

"Just go for it, Rosie!" she said.

Rose said okay, she would go for it.

Then Grace had to go, so they said goodbye and hung up.

Rose took a deep breath and headed to the front door. She had agreed to meet Mavis at their spot in the lot across the street so they could go over the plan to catch Henry.

On her way out, Rose heard her mother and Miss Jeeter in the kitchen talking about vichyssoise.

"It's supposed to be *cold*," her mother was saying. "Who ever heard of heating vichyssoise?"

"Cold?" Miss Jeeter snapped. "Who ever heard of cold soup?"

Rose could imagine the look on her mother's face when she heard that.

Then her mother started telling Miss Jeeter about the importance of washing leeks, but Rose wasn't interested. She went outside to meet Mavis.

"What are y'all doing?" Amanda hollered at them from her front porch.

Rose wanted to run away, but Mavis jutted her chin in the air and said, "Nothing."

"Yeah, right." Amanda stepped off the porch and came closer. She glanced back at her house and said in a low voice, "Y'all are looking for that dog."

"So?" Mavis said.

"So, if y'all are planning to catch that dog for Mr. Duffy, you're wasting your time."

"What do you mean?" Rose said.

Mavis headed toward the side of the house. "Just ignore her, Rose."

"What do you mean?" Rose repeated to Amanda.

"Everybody says Mr. Duffy is too old for that job," Amanda said. "I bet he's not going to be around much longer."

Rose felt her heart clench up tight. "Who says that?"

"Everybody."

"Don't listen to her, Rose," Mavis called from the side of the house.

But Rose *had* listened.

And now she had a stomachache.

But when Mavis called out, "Come on, Rose," she scrambled after her, pretending not to see Amanda standing there with her fists balled into her waist.

Then off they went into the woods, pushing through pricker bushes and climbing over fallen trees, searching for Henry.

MAVIS

"I think we're going too far," Rose called to Mavis. "I can hear the cars out on the highway. I'm not allowed to go near the highway."

Mavis stopped.

She turned around to face Rose and said, "No one will know. This'll be an adventure."

Personally, Mavis *loved* a good adventure, but she could tell that Rose did not.

"Come on, Rose," she said. "I bet you anything Henry is here somewhere."

"But we're going too far."

Mavis stomped her foot but immediately regretted it. She took a deep breath and said, "Okay. Then I'll just go on by myself."

Mavis turned and began to walk slowly in the direction of the highway. Then, imagine her surprise when she turned around and saw Rose heading back through the woods toward Magnolia Estates.

"Dang it," Mavis muttered to herself.

Suddenly this adventure didn't seem nearly as fun.

ROSE

Rose's feet felt like cement as she trudged up the street toward her house.

What was the matter with her, leaving Mavis alone in the woods like that? Why was she being such a scaredy-cat?

When she got home, she lifted her cement feet up the stairs to her room.

Clomp

Clomp

Clomp

Then she sat on her canopy bed and felt so heavy with shame that she was surprised she didn't sink right through the mattress and onto the floor.

Mavis was out there in the woods looking for Henry so that things would get right with Mr. Duffy.

Mavis knew how important Mr. Duffy was to her.

She was trying to make things better.

But here Rose sat, feeling so heavy. Acting like the baby that Amanda seemed to think she was.

Rose got up and went to her dresser. She opened the pink jewelry box with ROSE engraved in silver letters on the top. Nestled inside among the beaded necklaces and sparkly bracelets was Grace's silver dollar.

Rose held it in the palm of her hand and heard Grace say, "Just go for it, Rosie."

So she slipped the silver dollar into the pocket of her shorts and ran downstairs, out the door, down the driveway, and up the street to Amanda's house. Then she kept running along the wrought-iron fence and into the woods, calling Mavis's name.

MAVIS

Mavis couldn't believe it when she heard Rose calling her!

She stopped tromping through the woods and waited.

Sure enough, Rose came bursting through the tangled brush. When she caught her breath, she said, "Hey!"

Mavis grinned. "Hey."

Then Rose trudged right past Mavis, leading the way through the woods and calling for Henry.

As Mavis followed Rose, she felt like she was floating. Like her feet weren't even touching the leaf-covered ground or jumping over rotting branches.

Rose hadn't left her alone to carry out her plan by herself.

Rose was marching deeper into the woods, even though she wasn't allowed to be there.

Rose was being a very good best friend.

Mavis was so lost in those thoughts that she nearly jumped clean out of her sneakers when a thin white dog stepped out of a cluster of rhododendron and stopped right in front of her and Rose.

Henry!

She recognized that long thin nose. Those brown ears. That big brown spot on his side shaped like the map of Texas.

"Hey, fella," Mavis whispered.

Henry wagged his tail.

He was dirty as all get-out, with dark brown cockleburs stuck here and there in his fur.

"He's so skinny," Rose whispered.

Mavis took a step toward him. "It's okay, fella, I won't hurt you."

Henry backed up a little but wagged his tail.

Mavis took another step.

Wag, wag

Another step.

Wag, wag

Finally, Mavis was close enough to touch him. She reached out very slowly and put her hand on Henry's side, stroking him gently on that map-of-Texas brown spot. Next, she stroked his head, rubbing gently between his ears.

Then Mavis noticed something peculiar.

"Rose! Check this out!"

Henry had numbers on the underside of each ear!

Numbers!

Tattooed on his velvety ears.

Actually, one ear had three numbers and a letter: 117E. The other ear had five numbers: 51549.

What in the world could that mean? Why would a dog have numbers on his ears?

Mavis had never seen anything like it.

Rose took a few careful steps closer and peered down at Henry's ears. Then she looked at Mavis with wide eyes.

"Why does he have those numbers?" Mavis asked.

Rose shook her head. "I don't know, but I think he's a greyhound."

Mavis cocked her head and looked at Henry. "You think so?"

Rose nodded.

Henry nudged Mavis's hand with his long, skinny snout.

"We should've brought some treats," Mavis said. "I'm going to try to get him to come with us."

Then she reached for Henry with both hands.

But quick as lightning, he jerked away and took off running.

And in a blink, he was gone.

HENRY

Henry was feeling miserable.

He was tired of hiding in the woods. Prickers grabbed at his skin and roots made him stumble and wet leaves made for a cold bed at night.

His bad hip ached, slowing him down and making him limp.

He was hungry. The freckled girl didn't come to the fence as often as she used to, so the little plastic bowl was usually empty.

And then there were those two girls.

The quiet one and the wild-haired one.

Henry didn't know what to think about them.

Maybe he shouldn't have run away from Wonderland after all.

There was always food there.

And a warm, dry bed.

But something was different at Wonderland.

Something that did not feel right to Henry.

ROSE

Rose and Mavis sat on the log in the lot across the street. The morning dew still clung to the Queen Anne's lace at the edge of the woods. It was early, but already the midsummer sun beat down, making the air thick with heat.

Mavis was determined to catch Henry and take him to Mr. Duffy today. She was showing Rose how good she was at tying a slipknot in a piece of rope she had found in the garage. She explained how they could use it as a leash, and everything was going to be so easy.

Rose was glad her mother was getting her hair done and then meeting some ladies for lunch. If she saw Rose coming out of the woods with a dog, she would have a hissy fit.

"Let's go get some chicken or something from your kitchen," Mavis said.

"What for?"

"For Henry. So we can coax him out of wherever he's hiding."

"Oh." Rose knew Mavis wanted her to be excited, and she was trying. She really was.

She reached into her pocket and curled her fingers around Grace's silver dollar. Grace would've been so proud of her, running into the woods after Mavis like she had.

And hadn't Mavis been surprised? Rose could still see that grin on her face.

Rose took a deep breath and said, "Okay, let's go!"

And off she went, up the side of the street, with Mavis hollering, "Hey, wait for me!"

When they got to the back door, Mavis said, "Hopefully Mama's not in the kitchen. But if she is, let me handle it, okay?"

Rose gladly said, "Okay."

Mavis opened the kitchen door a crack and peeked in.

"She's not here," she whispered. "Come on."

The two of them tiptoed across the kitchen floor to the refrigerator.

Mavis began to root around inside.

"Roast beef!" she said. "And look at these!"

She showed Rose a plate of tiny quiches, like the ones Mrs. Tully often served when company came in the afternoon. Before Rose had a chance to tell Mavis she didn't think they should take those, Mavis had already dropped four of them into the plastic bag with the slices of roast beef.

"What's this?" Mavis pointed to something beside the plate of quiches.

Rose wrinkled her nose. "Liver pâté," she said. "It's nasty."

"Perfect!" Mavis said, and dropped it into the plastic bag.

"Mavis!"

Rose and Mavis jumped.

Mavis's mother stood in the doorway to the dining room with her hands on her hips.

And then Mavis did the most amazing thing.

Before she turned around to face her mother, she stuffed that plastic bag into the waist of her shorts and pulled her T-shirt down over it.

"Rose was hungry," Mavis said. "Right, Rose?" She poked Rose with her elbow.

Rose nodded, her face burning. *Why* was she so bad at lying? She'd give anything to be as good a liar as Mavis was.

Miss Jeeter narrowed her eyes and marched over to the refrigerator.

"Then y'all get some string cheese or something and get on out of here," she said. "I've got sheets to change upstairs."

Rose knew how much it annoyed Miss Jeeter to have to change the sheets so often. She had heard her grumbling under her breath that the Queen of England probably didn't have her sheets changed that often. So Rose knew that now was not a good time to be stealing food from the refrigerator.

But, of course, Mavis didn't care how annoyed her mother was. She was bound and determined to carry out her plan to catch Henry today no matter what.

"What about this?" Mavis held up a small plate of tomato aspic left over from last night's supper. Rose wanted to tell her that Henry probably wouldn't like tomato aspic, but Mavis's mother said, "Fine. Now take it and go."

Then, before Rose could tell Mavis that they at least needed forks for tomato aspic, Mavis was hurrying out the back door, calling, "Come on, Rose," behind her.

MAVIS

Mavis explained her perfect plan to Rose. They would go on back into the woods behind Amanda's house. They'd scatter the food around to lure Henry out of hiding. Then they'd use this rope for a leash and take Henry up to the gatehouse. Mr. Duffy would be so surprised! He would fall in love with Henry in no time flat.

Rose nodded.

Mavis put one of the tiny quiches beside a pine tree.

She put a slice of roast beef on a moss-covered log.

And she put some of the liver pâté by a clump of ferns.

"We should save the rest in case we need more," she said.

She motioned for Rose to come sit beside her in the damp leaves along the path.

Then they waited.

And waited.

And waited.

Just when Mavis was going to suggest that they go to another spot, a dog's long thin white nose appeared from behind a shrub.

The nose was sniffing.

Next, a dog's brown and white head appeared.

Henry's head.

He looked at Rose and Mavis.

His nose kept sniffing.

He hurried to the moss-covered log and gobbled up the roast beef.

Then the liver pâté by the ferns.

Then the quiche beside the pine tree.

Then he walked right over to Rose and Mavis and sat down.

"Hey, Henry," Mavis said softly. She ran her hand gently over the top of his head. "Look what I have."

She opened the plastic bag in her lap and showed Henry the food inside. Then she took out another one of those quiches and held it in the palm of her hand.

Henry snatched it off and swallowed it in one big gulp.

Then Mavis made her move. She dropped the rope with the perfect slipknot over his head.

Henry flinched and then pulled, causing the rope to tighten. At first he looked so scared that Mavis felt bad.

She quickly began to comfort him, telling him what a good boy he was and rubbing his sides. Then she gave him a piece of roast beef and was glad to see that he looked calmer. He stopped pulling on the rope and sat between Rose and Mavis and ate the rest of the roast beef and even the tomato aspic right out of the plastic bag.

After the food was gone, he lay down, put his head on his paws, and let out a doggy sigh.

"Aw, he's so sweet," Rose said.

"I know." Mavis grinned at Rose. "We did it!"

Then they did their special handshake, slapping, snapping, and fist-bumping.

"Come on," Mavis said. "Let's take him to Mr. Duffy."

ROSE

It was true that Rose had done the special handshake when they caught Henry, but deep down inside, she had been hoping that Mavis's plan wouldn't work.

She knew that wasn't very nice, but it was true.

And just the thought made Grace's silver dollar grow heavy in her pocket. Why couldn't she be happy they had finally caught Henry? But Rose being Rose, she couldn't stop her worried thoughts from creeping in and planting questions.

Like: How in the world could they get Henry out of the woods and up to the gatehouse without somebody seeing them? And what if that somebody was nosy Amanda? Even worse, what if that somebody was her mother?

So even while she was slapping and snapping and fist-bumping with Mavis, Rose was feeling a little sorry that the plan had worked.

But here she was, running along behind Mavis with Henry, hoping and praying that nobody saw them.

As they ran beside Amanda's wrought-iron fence, Rose kept her eyes on the ground, not daring to look up and see Amanda standing in her yard.

Then, as they ran up the edge of the road, Rose's heart nearly thumped clean out of her chest while she said a little prayer that her mother's shiny black car would not appear.

But besides her thumping heart, Rose had a little niggle.

A niggle about Henry.

There was something about Henry that was bothering her.

Something that she thought she should maybe tell Mavis about.

When they reached the gatehouse, Rose said, "Um, Mavis . . ."

But Mavis opened the screen door and said, "Okay, cross your fingers. Here we go."

When Mavis stepped through the door with Henry, Rose hollered, "Wait! I think—"

But Mavis and Henry had already disappeared inside.

Rose crossed her fingers and stepped inside behind them.

HENRY

Henry had made a big mistake.

He should've ignored that delicious food and stayed hidden in the bushes.

He never should have trusted this wild-haired girl.

He should've run far away from that wrought-iron fence where the freckled girl lived.

He should've run farther away from Wonderland.

But he hadn't.

Now here he was, inside a small building with a gray-haired man who looked quite surprised.

MAVIS

"Ta-da!" Mavis said, sweeping her arm out toward Henry.

"What in the name of sweet Bessie McGee is *that*?" Mr. Duffy stared at Henry.

Mavis grinned. "A dog!" she said. "A really sweet dog who needs a home. Right, Rose?"

Rose looked from Mr. Duffy to Henry and back to Mr. Duffy. "Um, right."

"I know he's kind of funny-looking," Mavis said. "So skinny. But he's nice."

"Where in tarnation did y'all find that mongrel?" Mr. Duffy walked slowly around the gatehouse, inspecting Henry from a distance.

Henry sat beside Mavis, watching Mr. Duffy, looking kind of pitiful.

"In the woods," Mavis said. "He's been there for a long time. That's why he's so skinny. He needs a home, right, Rose?"

Rose nodded.

"And he has tattoos on his ears," Mavis said. "I bet you never saw *that* before."

Mr. Duffy raised his eyebrows. "Tattoos?"

"Yeah, look." Mavis flipped Henry's ears over and showed Mr. Duffy the tattoos.

117E

51549

Mr. Duffy squinted down at Henry's ears. Then he straightened up, took his cap off, scratched the top of his head, and said, "That dog's from Wonderland."

ROSE

"Wonderland?" Mavis said.

"Yep." Mr. Duffy put his cap back on and nodded toward Henry. "That dog's from Wonderland, or my name ain't Duffy."

"What's Wonderland?" Mavis asked.

But Rose knew what Wonderland was.

Which is why she had had that little niggle about Henry.

Mr. Duffy jerked his head toward the door. "Dog track up yonder on the other side of the highway," he said.

"What's a dog track?" Mavis asked.

But Rose knew what a dog track was.

Rose knew because her uncle AJ went there and

wasted his hard-earned money. At least, that's what Rose's mother always said.

"It's humiliating to know that my own brother goes to that dog track and wastes his hard-earned money," she often snapped when Uncle AJ came over.

Mr. Duffy explained Wonderland to Mavis. How the dogs raced around a track, chasing a stuffed rabbit on a pole. How people went to Wonderland to watch the dogs race and to bet money on them. How Henry must have run away from Wonderland and how he would have to go back.

Mavis's face fell. "But how do you know he came from there?" she said.

"It's as plain as the tail on a rattler," Mr. Duffy said. "He's a greyhound, for one thing. And those ear tattoos, for another. Sure sign of a racer."

"What do they mean?" Mavis rubbed the numbers on Henry's ears.

"I'm not exactly sure, but I've seen plenty of 'em." Mr. Duffy went over to his desk and dropped into his chair with a groan. "I tossed away more than a few dollars at that track back when I was young and dumb."

"You did?" Mavis said.

Mr. Duffy nodded. "I sure did. And Edna? Sweet-as-pecan-pie Edna? She'd get mad as all get-out. Wouldn't say pea turkey squat to me for days."

Mavis kissed Henry on his nose. He must've liked being kissed, because he snuggled against her shoulder and licked her on the cheek.

"Aren't you going to keep him?" Mavis asked.

Mr. Duffy shook his head. "That dog's not mine to keep," he said. "He's gotta go back to where he came from."

And that was that.

Mr. Duffy called Wonderland to come and get Henry.

MAVIS

Mavis couldn't believe her plan hadn't worked. She had been so sure everything was going to turn out great.

But it hadn't.

So here she was, sitting outside the gatehouse with Rose, waiting on someone from Wonderland to come and pick up Henry.

"I wonder if he wins a lot of races," Rose said, patting the top of Henry's head. "I bet he does."

Suddenly Mavis snapped her fingers. "Hey, we should go there sometime!"

"Where?"

"To Wonderland."

Rose shook her head. "My mother doesn't approve of

Wonderland. My uncle AJ goes there and loses a lot of money."

"We could go to watch sometime," Mavis said. "We wouldn't even have to tell anybody. It could be like our first Best Friends Club field trip."

Rose got that worried look that Mavis knew well.

"Forget it, then," Mavis said. "I'll go by myself."

Rose didn't answer, so Mavis said it again.

"I'll go by myself."

Then, just as Mavis was starting to get irritated, a white van pulled up to the gatehouse. Painted on the side in black letters was:

WONDERLAND GREYHOUND PARK

PALMETTO ROAD

LANDRY, ALABAMA

A bald-headed man wearing a red Wonderland T-shirt got out of the van. Over the pocket of his shirt was the name Roger. "Well, you little devil," he said to Henry. "We been looking all over for you."

Henry put his tail between his legs and hung his head.

Then the man slipped a collar and leash over Henry's head and said, "Thanks for calling me, y'all."

Before Mavis even had a chance to hug Henry

goodbye, the man scooped him up and put him into a crate in the back of the van.

"Bye, Henry," Mavis called.

"Bye, Henry," Rose called.

The man climbed into the driver's seat, draped his arm out the window, and gave Rose and Mavis a wave.

"Can we come watch him race sometime?" Mavis asked as the van was backing away from the gatehouse.

"This one ain't racing no more," the man said.

Then the van drove off, leaving a puff of black smoke behind it.

ROSE

"Wait! Stop!"

Mavis was running after the van.

But it didn't stop.

It kept going until it disappeared from sight.

Mavis stopped running and stomped her foot. "Dang it!"

Rose ran to catch up with her.

"What's wrong?" she said.

"What's wrong? Didn't you hear what that man said?"

"About what?"

"About Henry."

"Um, I . . ."

Mavis gestured in the direction where the van had disappeared. "He said Henry doesn't race anymore."

"So?"

"So why is he there?"

"Well, I guess he, well, um . . ."

"We have to go there," Mavis said.

Rose had a bad feeling that Mavis was about to talk her into doing something she wouldn't want to do.

"Go where?" she asked.

But she knew the answer.

"Wonderland," Mavis said, throwing her arms out and then dropping them with a loud slap against her legs.

Yep, Rose had been right. Mavis was going to try to convince her to go to Wonderland. But that would be crazy. In fact, that would be the craziest thing Rose had ever done.

Crazier than going back in those woods where she wasn't supposed to go.

Crazier than taking those little quiches her mother always kept for company.

Crazier than bringing Henry to Mr. Duffy.

"Don't you get it?" Mavis said. "If Henry isn't racing anymore, then what's he doing there? What happens to the dogs who don't race? Maybe they get sent to a dog pound or something. Let's go find out."

"How are we gonna go to Wonderland? I don't even know for sure where it is, but I know it's way on the other side of the highway. I'm not even allowed to go *near* the highway."

"We'll ride bikes. We can do it."

Then Mavis started rambling on and on about how they would go to Wonderland and find Henry.

Mavis always made everything sound so easy.

Suddenly there were two Roses.

One Rose wanted to say, "No."

She wanted to say, "Forget it."

She wanted to go back home and sit in Grace's room by herself.

But the other Rose wanted to do their special hand-shake and say, "Let's go for it!"

But both Roses just stood there, listening to Mavis make everything sound so easy.

MAVIS

"Geez, you would've thought I'd committed a crime or something," Mavis's mother said as she took pizza out of the microwave. "It looked like a sugar bowl to me. How was I supposed to know it was for salt?"

She cut the pizza into slices and dropped one onto a paper plate for Mavis.

"Who ever heard of a salt cellar, anyway?" she said.

While Mavis ate her pizza, her mother went on and on about Mrs. Tully.

How she'd gotten so irritated when her mother didn't know how to cook artichokes.

And who cares whether you serve the chicken platter from the left or the right?

And what's the point of having dishes that you can't even put in the dishwasher?

But Mavis wasn't listening.

She was thinking.

Could she convince Rose to go with her to Wonderland?

If she could, where would they get another bicycle? Mavis had only seen one in the garage.

If they did get another bicycle, would they be able to find Wonderland?

And if they did, could they get in?

If they got in, would Henry still be there?

So many questions.

ROSE

When the "Ode to Joy" doorbell rang, Rose opened the front door, and there was Amanda Simm.

"I'm selling raffle tickets for my swim team," Amanda said. "To raise money for our meet in Birmingham."

"How much are they?" Rose asked.

"They're five dollars each, and there are a bunch of prizes, including a weekend time-share condo in the Smoky Mountains," Amanda said. "Will you ask your mom?"

"Um, sure. Just a minute."

Rose found her mother on the screened porch, reading, and told her about Amanda's raffle tickets. Her mother said she would buy five.

When Rose returned to the front door with the money, Amanda thanked her and turned to leave.

"Wait!" Rose said.

Amanda waited.

"Um . . ." Rose shifted from one foot to the other. In her head, she argued with herself.

Ask her.

Don't ask her.

Ask her.

Don't ask her.

And then she did.

"Can Mavis and I borrow your bike?" she asked.

Amanda narrowed her eyes. "What for?"

"Um, just to ride."

"Ride where?"

Then Rose argued with herself again.

Fib.

Don't fib.

Fib.

Don't fib.

And then she did.

"To ride around Magnolia Estates," she fibbed. "Maybe we could come to some of your swim meets."

Amanda cocked her head and had *skeptical* written all over her face. If she didn't answer soon, Rose was going to slam the door and run up to Grace's room.

But then Amanda said, "Sure. I guess so."

Rose couldn't wait to tell Mavis that she had asked Amanda about borrowing her bike. She was so proud of herself that she called Grace and told her about Mavis's crazy plan to go to Wonderland.

"No way!" Grace said.

"Yes, way!"

"Rosie, that's awesome," Grace said. "I'm so glad you have a friend like Mavis."

"Yeah, me too."

But of course, Rose didn't tell Grace that she didn't really *want* to go to Wonderland. That the thought of riding her bike across the highway gave her a stomachache. That she could never be as brave and adventurous as Mavis was.

That evening, the Magnolia Estates Garden Club sat on the Tullys' patio, sipping sweet tea and talking about Mr. Duffy.

Rose sat on the window seat in Grace's room and listened with a knot of dread growing inside her.

"Sometimes I wonder if he's going deaf," one lady said. "I specifically told him my niece was coming last Tuesday, and he swears up and down I never did."

"When Wanda Lawrence came to hang my new drapes," another lady said, "she told me he had been *sleeping* when she stopped at the gatehouse."

The others mumbled things like "good heavens" and "seriously?"

Rose could picture them down there, nibbling on their quiches and nodding at one another.

And it made her feel terrible when she realized they were right.

But was Mavis right?

If Mr. Duffy had another dog to love, would he really be like his old self again?

And could he ever love Henry the way he had loved Queenie?

But that didn't matter anyway because Henry belonged at Wonderland.

Still, Mavis had a point.

If Henry wasn't racing, why was he there?

Then one of the ladies down on the patio said, "Well, personally, I think it's time to discuss Mr. Duffy at our next board meeting."

Those words hit Rose hard.

Like a punch.

So she made a decision right then and there.

She would go to Wonderland with Mavis.

HENRY

When the bald man named Roger opened the crate and let Henry out of the van, the dog's heart sank.

Just as he had suspected.

He was back at Wonderland.

Henry didn't understand what was going on in the place where he had lived his whole life.

First of all, he wasn't racing anymore.

Why?

He had been racing for as long as he could remember.

And now he wasn't.

Maybe he wasn't quite as fast as he used to be.

Maybe that bad hip of his made him limp sometimes.

But still, racing was what he had always done.

And now he wasn't.

And second of all, he had been moved out of the kennels where he had always lived.

Now he was in a new building, where every few days one of the dogs left and didn't come back.

Where were they going? Why weren't they coming back? Maybe something bad was happening to them.

Henry felt scared and confused.

He was convinced he shouldn't stay here in this new place.

He would wait for just the right time.

Then he would run away again.

MAVIS

It had been raining for three days.

Mavis was bored.

She and Rose had been to the gatehouse every day.

Sometimes the three of them played cards, but most of the time they stared out at the rain, which left little rivers running along the edges of the streets of Magnolia Estates. The heat left the gatehouse windows cloudy with steam and the air smelling like mildew.

Mavis couldn't wait until she and Rose went to Wonderland.

If only the rain would stop.

And, speaking of Rose, Mavis could hardly believe that she had convinced Amanda to let them borrow her bike. Such an un-Rose-like thing to do!

But Mavis was a little worried that Rose might change her mind about going to Wonderland. The more it rained, the more Mavis worried. She also worried that if they waited much longer, Henry might be gone. Since he didn't race anymore, would he still be at Wonderland? And if he wasn't, where would he be?

Mavis had never been a worrier.

But now she was.

Not as much as Rose, of course, but still . . .

If only it would stop raining so she and Rose could go to Wonderland.

ROSE

Rose had two feelings twirling around together.

First of all, she was feeling pretty proud of herself for asking Amanda if she and Mavis could borrow her bike.

Maybe she really was getting to be more like Mavis.

But twirling around with *that* feeling was another one.

Guilt.

Rose was feeling guilty that she didn't want the rain to stop.

Sure, she had agreed to go to Wonderland.

But now that she had committed to going, she wasn't feeling quite so sure.

As long as it rained, she wouldn't have to actually do it.

She could hang out in the gatehouse with Mr. Duffy instead.

The problem with that, though, was that it seemed like he was getting grumpier every day.

When Mildred Owings had called to complain about Mr. Duffy letting somebody selling magazine subscriptions into Magnolia Estates, he had practically hung up on her. Then he'd grumbled about her all morning.

"That woman is so annoying she could make a preacher cuss," he'd said, not once, but three times.

When Darlene Badger had stopped by to take a look at his clipboard to make sure the guests for her barbecue were on there, he had handed it to her with a big *humph*.

After she'd left, Mr. Duffy had said, "She thinks she can charm the dew right off the honeysuckle."

When the rain didn't let up, Mavis got more and more impatient.

"Maybe we should go anyway," she said. "Who cares about a little rain?"

But finally the day came.

The rain stopped.

The sun came out, drying up the puddles and making the raindrops on the dogwood tree beneath Rose's bedroom window sparkle like diamonds. Steam drifted up off the Tullys' winding driveway, and Monroe Tucker showed up to mow the lawn.

Rose knew Mavis would be waiting for her at the back door. That had been their plan. To meet at the back door as soon as it stopped raining.

Rose tiptoed into the hallway and listened. Was her mother home? She hoped not. If her mother saw her taking her bike out of the garage, she would be suspicious. Rose never rode her bike.

Suddenly Miss Jeeter came into the foyer with a feather duster, singing. That was a good sign. Miss Jeeter would never sing if Rose's mother had been home.

So Rose hurried down the stairs, gave a quick wave to Miss Jeeter, and went out the back door.

Sure enough, there was Mavis.

Rose hadn't even made it to the bottom of the steps when Mavis dashed toward the garage hollering, "Get your bike. We're going to Wonderland!"

MAVIS

Mavis couldn't remember the last time she'd had such an adventure.

Once, back in Georgia, when Jonelle Bolt was sleeping over, they had sneaked out of the house after her mother went to bed and gone up to the 7-Eleven to buy candy. But on the way back home, the cops had stopped them and told them that two little girls shouldn't be out alone so late at night. They had taken Jonelle and her home in their patrol car and then woken her mother up. Hoo boy, *that* had been a scene. No wonder Jonelle never wanted to come over to her house again.

But that had been nothing compared to this adventure.

Amanda had agreed to leave her bike for them beside

her garage, so now Rose and Mavis were walking the bikes through the woods on their way to the highway. Rose had a million questions, and Mavis had an answer for every one of them.

How were they going to get across the highway?

Easy. They'd walk along the edge until they got to a stoplight.

How were they going to find Palmetto Road?

No problem. There weren't that many roads in Landry. It shouldn't be hard.

What were they going to do when they got to Wonderland?

They'd find somebody in charge and tell them they wanted to see Henry.

On and on and on.

A million questions.

Mavis led the way, pushing Amanda's bike through the woods, weaving in and out of prickery brush and occasionally lifting the bike over fallen trees, until they reached a clearing. There, below a grassy ravine, was the highway.

Her insides swirled with excitement.

But one look at Rose told her that Rose's insides were not swirling with excitement. Rose looked like she was ready to turn her bike around and head for home any minute.

Mavis knew she had to act fast.

"Come on," she said. "Let's ride down to where the stoplight is."

Then she jumped on the bike and pedaled as fast as she could down the ravine and along the edge of the highway. Every now and then she glanced behind her to make sure Rose was following.

"Hurry up!" she called to Rose, who was falling farther and farther behind.

When she got to the stoplight, she waited for Rose to catch up.

If everything went according to her plan, they would find Wonderland over there on the other side of the highway. Then they would find out where Henry was.

She was sure that everything about her plan was perfect.

ROSE

As Rose pedaled hard to keep up with Mavis, she once again had that feeling that there were two Roses.

One was the scared Rose.

Scared to be here riding her bicycle along the edge of the busy highway, with cars zooming by so fast the wild-flowers danced in the breeze when they passed.

Scared that her mother was going to find out about this very un-Rose-like thing she was doing.

Scared that even if they found Henry, and even if Henry needed a home, Mr. Duffy wouldn't want him and would be unhappy with her. Mr. Duffy had never been unhappy with her before.

But then there was another Rose.

A Rose who was thrilled with this wild adventure.

A Rose who was as brave as her best friend, Mavis.

A Rose who wished her sister could see her now.

But when she finally caught up with Mavis and found herself crossing the busy highway at the stoplight, that second Rose quickly disappeared.

Why had she let Mavis talk her into this?

But it was too late to turn back now. They were already across the highway, and Mavis was hollering, "Follow me!"

And so she did.

She followed Mavis up one street and down another.

Through neighborhoods with small brick houses and tidy yards where kids playing in the street stared at them when they pedaled by.

Past a car repair shop, a tattoo parlor, a florist, and a barber shop.

Past Brookhaven Baptist Church and Patton Road Car Wash and Miss Banner's Daycare Center.

Then they turned a corner, and suddenly Mavis squealed, "There it is!"

Sure enough, looming ahead was a large sign reading WONDERLAND GREYHOUND PARK.

Mavis let out a whoop and motioned for Rose to

follow her through the empty parking lot and right up to the entrance gate beside the ticket booth.

Mavis jumped off her bike and jiggled the gate.

Locked.

Rose felt a wave of relief wash over her.

"It's closed," she said to Mavis. "We should leave."

"No way. There're people in there."

Rose peered through the fence. Inside the park were folks wearing red caps or T-shirts with WONDERLAND on them. Some were walking dogs that looked a lot like Henry.

"Hey!" Mavis called through the gate.

No one seemed to notice.

"We should leave," Rose said again, glancing back in the direction of the highway.

She reached into her pocket and rubbed Grace's silver dollar.

Mavis waved and hollered at folks inside Wonderland until finally some woman with a bushy gray ponytail under her Wonderland cap came to the gate and asked Mavis what she wanted.

"We're looking for a dog," Mavis said.

"A rescue dog?" the woman asked.

Mavis's face lit up. "Yes! A rescue dog. Right, Rose?"

Rose nodded.

"Do you have an appointment?" the woman asked.

Rose couldn't believe her ears when Mavis said, "Yes."

Mavis sure was a good fibber. She didn't even look one bit guilty. Rose felt a wave of admiration.

The woman unlocked the gate, and, just like that, Rose and Mavis were inside Wonderland.

MAVIS

Mavis could hardly believe how great this adventure was turning out.

She had actually found Wonderland.

And now she had convinced someone to let them in.

Wonderland was a hustle-bustle of activity. Everywhere Mavis looked were dogs.

Dogs on leashes.

Dogs in kennels.

Dogs playing in grassy fenced areas.

And all the dogs looked a lot like Henry, with long skinny legs and long pointy noses.

Mavis kept saying to Rose, "Isn't this cool?" and "Did you see that?"

Rose would nod or shrug.

Mavis wished that Rose were having as much fun as she was, but it didn't seem like she was.

The woman with the bushy gray ponytail led them to a cinder-block building.

"Here ya go," she said.

Mavis leaned her bike against the building and went inside, motioning for Rose to do the same.

Inside, the air was damp and smelled like dogs. Along each side were rows of kennels. Inside most of the kennels was a barking dog. A greyhound, like Henry. At the end of each kennel was a small door that led to an outside kennel.

Roger, the man who had picked Henry up in the van, was washing metal bowls.

"Can I help y'all?" he said. "I don't have any appointments until tomorrow."

"We're looking for a dog," Mavis told him.

"Got an appointment?" Roger asked.

"Um . . ." Mavis couldn't think of a good fib, so she said, "We're looking for that white dog with a brown spot on his side."

"Ah, y'all are the ones who found that rascal who ran off." The man dried his hands on his jeans.

Mavis nodded. "His name is Henry and we found him

and he really loves us, but Mr. Duffy called to have him picked up. Right, Rose?"

Rose nodded.

Roger chuckled. "His name is Alabama Rocket Boy, and he's a naughty one."

Alabama Rocket Boy?

What kind of name was that for a dog?

"Can we see him?" Mavis asked.

Roger led them down the row of kennels. When they got to the last one, which was empty, Roger whistled.

Sure enough, Henry came leaping through the little door from outside and darted over to the front of the kennel, wagging his tail and whining with excitement at the sight of Rose and Mavis.

"Hey, Henry!" Mavis said, stooping and putting her hand through the chain link for him to sniff.

Henry wagged his tail so hard his whole body wagged.

"He remembers us!" Mavis said.

Rose ran her hand along Henry's nose.

Mavis told Roger how she and Rose had found Henry in the woods and taken him to Mr. Duffy.

"We wanted Mr. Duffy to keep him, but he said Henry belonged here."

"Well, if one of y'all wants a dog, you've come to the

right place," Roger said. "Ole Rocket Boy here is ready for adoption."

"He is?" Mavis turned to Rose. "See? I *told* you. I *knew* it."

Then she turned back to Roger and said. "We'll take him."

Rose gave her a wide-eyed look and said, "But—"

"You can't just take him," Roger said.

Mavis stood up. "Why not?"

Roger told Rose and Mavis about the Wonderland Adoption Center.

The dogs were greyhounds who had lived their whole lives right here at the racetrack. They had been trained to run since they were puppies. When they were ready to race, they lived in the race kennels.

But by the time the dogs were three or four years old, they were too old to race anymore.

"Too old?" Mavis said.

"Yep. They slow down, like Rocket Boy." He nodded toward Henry. "He's got a bum hip, too. A few years of hard racing will do that sometimes."

"What happens to them when they get too old?"

"They're ready for adoption," Roger said. "I try my best to find 'em a good home."

"Really?" Mavis looked at Rose. "Then we'll adopt him, right, Rose?"

"Whoa now," Roger said. "It don't happen like that. For one thing, y'all have to have a grown-up with you. And then there's paperwork and interviews and home inspections and stuff."

Mavis felt her shoulders droop. All her careful planning hadn't included this.

Now what?

How could she and Rose get Henry and Mr. Duffy together?

ROSE

Rose sat at the breakfast table thinking about Wonderland. She tried to keep her mouth from smiling, but she could feel the corners twitching, just dying to grin at the very thought of it.

She could hardly believe she had actually done it.

Ridden her bike *across the highway*.

Gone to Wonderland.

Gone *inside* Wonderland.

And found Henry.

Rose's insides were dancing with the giddiness of this amazing thing she had done.

Maybe she was starting to become like Mavis.

Or at least a little bit like Mavis.

Sure of herself and brave.

Well, sort of sure of herself and kind of brave.

Rose couldn't wait to call Grace and tell her all about it.

"What's so funny, Rose?" her mother asked, jolting Rose out of her happy Wonderland thoughts.

"Nothing." Rose forced her starting-to-smile mouth to straighten out and concentrate on the French toast on her plate.

"Brenda Putnam is organizing a mother-daughter book club for Magnolia Estates," her mother said.

Rose swirled her fork around in the puddle of maple syrup on her plate and thunked her heels against the legs of her chair. She stared at her plate, knowing her mother would have that familiar look of disapproval on her face.

"Are Mavis and Miss Jeeter going to join?" she asked.

Her mother took a sip of grapefruit juice and said, "Um, well, of course not."

Rose looked up. "Why not?"

"The club is for Magnolia Estates, Rose."

"But they live in Magnolia Estates."

Her mother glared at the newspaper Mr. Tully held in front of his face, sending lasers of disapproval at his silence.

Mr. Tully cleared his throat and turned to a new page of the paper.

Mrs. Tully set her fork carefully on the edge of her plate, leaned forward, and whispered, "Please, Rose, Miss Jeeter is in the kitchen and might hear you."

Rose was surprised to feel that tiny seed of bravery she had been feeling earlier begin to grow. She sat up straight and said, "If it's a club for mothers and daughters who live in Magnolia Estates, then that means every mother and daughter."

She glanced over at her father, who lowered the newspaper and winked at her.

Rose winked back, then turned to her mother and said, "Right?"

Rose felt herself smiling.

She felt herself being confident and brave.

She felt herself being like Mavis.

But then this scene of amazing bravery was interrupted when Mr. Tully excused himself to grab his briefcase and head to work.

Miss Jeeter burst through the swinging door from the kitchen to gather the breakfast dishes.

Mrs. Tully sat red-faced and silent.

And Rose swiped her finger through the maple syrup on her plate, licked it off with a loud slurp, and headed outside to meet Mavis.

Today they were going to tell Mr. Duffy that he could adopt Henry.

HENRY

Henry had been glad to see those two girls again.

The wild-haired one and the quiet one.

It was true that they had tricked him with that food and taken him to the gray-haired man.

It was true that he had ended up back here in Wonderland.

But when those girls showed up, soothing him and petting him, Henry thought maybe they had come to take him away.

But no.

They had left without him.

Henry lay down in the corner of his kennel and put his nose on his paws, feeling very sad.

Some of the dogs around him barked and howled. And some of them sat quietly, looking bored.

Before long, Roger came to take them outside to play in one of the grassy fenced areas beside the kennels. The one with the fence that was bent and loose.

Now was Henry's chance. He would look for that loose place in the fence. Then he would crawl under it until he was free on the other side.

Henry's heart raced. Would that place in the fence still be there? Maybe someone had seen it and fixed it. Maybe he wouldn't be able to get out again.

When Henry and the other dogs got into the grassy area, some of them began to run excitedly from one end to the other. Some of them began to play with one another. But Henry walked along the fence, looking for the spot where he had escaped. He had to hurry. Their time in the play yard was never very long.

And then he found it. That place in the fence that was bent and loose, exactly the way it had been before.

He nudged the fencing with his nose and lifted it enough to squeeze under and out the other side.

Then he ran and ran and ran, not looking back.

MAVIS

"I think he's *sleeping*," Mavis said to Rose when they got to the gatehouse.

Sure enough, Mr. Duffy was sitting in his chair with his feet on the desk and his cap pulled down over his eyes. His mouth was open, and he breathed in with a rumbly snore and exhaled with a *whoosh*.

Mavis slowly opened the screen door and stepped inside, with Rose following close behind. "Should we wake him up?" she whispered.

Rose nodded.

Mavis went, "*Ahem*," and let the screen door slam shut with a bang.

Mr. Duffy bolted straight up and looked wildly around him. When he saw Rose and Mavis, he clutched his heart and said, "Jeekers! Y'all trying to scare me to kingdom come and back?"

"Sorry," Rose said.

"We have some great news," Mavis said. "Right, Rose?"

Rose nodded. "Great news."

Mr. Duffy put his feet on the floor and straightened his cap. "Lay it on me," he said. "I could use some great news."

"Tell him, Rose," Mavis said, giving Rose a little nudge.

"Well, um, Henry, you know, that dog? Well, Mavis and I went to Wonderland and, he, um, we found out—"

"Henry is up for *adoption*!" Mavis blurted out. "Can you believe that?"

Mr. Duffy squinted at them. "Now, what in tarnation are y'all talking about? Please tell me y'all did *not* go over there to that racetrack." He shook his head. "No sirree bob, that is *not* the truth."

He ducked his head and lifted his bushy gray eyebrows. "Miss Rose Tully?"

Rose blushed and looked down at the floor.

"I *know* what your mama would think about that," he said. "That is not like you one bit to go and do such a dern fool crazy thing."

"But it turned out great, right, Rose?" Mavis said, grinning.

Mr. Duffy snorted. "Two little ole girls like y'all going over there to that track?" He poked a finger at Rose and said, "You can't keep trouble from coming, but you don't have to give it a chair to sit on."

Rose looked like she was about to cry, staring down at the floor with her chin quivering.

Mavis put her arm around Rose. "But she *didn't* get in trouble 'cause her mama doesn't know. And here's the best part." She pushed a tangle of hair out of her eyes. "You can adopt Henry!" She gave Rose's shoulder a little jiggle and grinned at Mr. Duffy.

Then the room got so quiet that Mavis could hear some kids hollering "Not it!" somewhere up the street.

Think fast, Mavis told herself. Her plan was almost working. Now was her chance. So Mavis did what she knew how to do best. She jumped right in and tried to make things right. She told Mr. Duffy about Wonderland.

How some lady had showed them the way to the cinder-block building.

How that man named Roger had told them about Henry. That he was only four years old but that was too old to race, so he was ready to be adopted.

"*And*," Mavis added, "he even told us what those ear tattoos mean."

Mr. Duffy sat there at his desk, not saying a word while Mavis explained the tattoos. "The one on his left ear is his identification number with the National Greyhound Association," she said. "And the one on his right ear identifies exactly which puppy he is in his litter. So every dog has different numbers. How about that?"

Mr. Duffy took his cap off and scratched his head. "Guess you're never too old to learn something new," he said.

"*And*," Mavis went on, "Henry would be perfect for you. He's smart and sweet and—"

Mr. Duffy held up a hand and said, "Whoa, now, missy. That dog don't need an old geezer like me. I know I sound like my heart's a thumping gizzard, but—"

"A what?" Mavis said.

Mr. Duffy chuckled. "Thumping gizzard. Means y'all must think I'm coldhearted and—"

"I don't," Rose chimed in.

"Me, neither," Mavis said.

"Well, anyway," Mr. Duffy continued, "I'm not looking for another dog, so you two schemers can stop right here and now, and that's final."

Mavis looked at Rose and Rose looked at Mavis and they both looked at Mr. Duffy, who repeated, "Final."

And then an appliance repair truck pulled up to the gatehouse, and Mr. Duffy said, "Now y'all let me get back to work before one of those old biddies starts flinging complaints my way."

So Rose and Mavis headed back up the street toward the Tullys' house. When they reached the driveway, Mavis slapped a hand on Rose's shoulder and said, "Don't worry. I will *not* give up. I'll come up with plan B. I'm really good at that."

ROSE

Rose sat on Grace's window seat feeling bad.

Mr. Duffy had scolded her for going to Wonderland.

He had never scolded her before.

Of course, she had never done anything like going to Wonderland before.

Riding her bike across that highway that she wasn't even allowed to go *near*.

And going inside that racetrack where her uncle AJ went, making her mother so aggravated with him.

She had hoped maybe Mr. Duffy would think she was brave and adventurous, like Mavis.

But instead, he had said she had given trouble a chair to sit on.

Rose lay down on the window seat and rested her

head on the heart-shaped pillow that Grace had made in home economics class in high school. It still had the faint scent of that lavender talcum powder Grace loved so much.

Rose wished Mr. Duffy wouldn't talk about being an old geezer.

And that he wouldn't say his heart was a thumping gizzard.

She wished Mavis's plan had worked.

That Mr. Duffy would adopt Henry.

And be happy again.

And not fall asleep in the gatehouse or let magazine salespeople into Magnolia Estates.

But Mavis's plan had not worked.

Rose hoped more than anything that Mavis really was good at coming up with plan B.

MAVIS

"Rose said there's going to be a mother-daughter book club, and you and I can be in it," Mavis said.

Her mother didn't answer.

She didn't open her eyes.

She sat in the chair in the corner of the apartment with her feet up on the end of the bed and her head on a pillow.

"Mama," Mavis said.

No answer.

"Mama!" Mavis yelled.

Her mother opened her eyes.

"Seriously, May?" she said. "Seriously?"

She lifted her feet with a grunt and dropped them to the floor like they were sacks of rocks. Then she leaned forward with her hands on her knees and said, "You're kidding me, right?"

"No," Mavis said. "I am *not* kidding."

"A mother-daughter book club."

Mavis nodded.

Her mother dropped back in the chair and shook her head.

"Mavis," she said, "mother-daughter book clubs are for mothers and daughters who eat cold soup and use a dang silver spoon for their salt instead of a salt shaker like the rest of the world. Mother-daughter book clubs are for mothers who need clean sheets every other day and daughters who belong to the Junior Garden Club."

She leaned forward again and jabbed a finger in Mavis's direction. "Mother-daughter book clubs are not for you and me."

Mavis felt anger working its way up from the bottom of her feet to the top of her head.

"Why do you have to be so mad about everything every minute of the day?" she hollered. "Every time we move somewhere new you say you're going to like it better, but you never do. You just have something new to gripe about."

Mavis stalked to the door. "Well, I like it here, and

Rose is my best friend," she said, yanking the screen door open and stepping out onto the little porch. "And she does *not* belong to the Junior Garden Club," she yelled through the door before stomping down the steps.

Maybe her mother thought they weren't good enough for that stupid book club, but Rose didn't think so because she had *invited* them.

Mavis had a bad feeling about her mother and Mrs. Tully. It seemed like all they did was argue. It seemed like Mrs. Tully thought her mother did everything wrong. And it seemed like all her mother ever did was complain about Mrs. Tully.

Mavis got Rose's skateboard out of the garage and went around front to the driveway. She wasn't allowed to ride the skateboard on the driveway anymore. Mrs. Tully didn't like it. But the Tullys weren't home. They were going to some fancy restaurant over in Mobile. Rose had told her it would be boring and she wished she could stay home with Mavis.

"Really?" Mavis had said.

Rose had looked surprised and said a very un-Rose-like thing.

"Well, duh!" she had said, holding out her palm so they could do their special handshake.

Slapping, snapping, and fist-bumping.

Now Mavis rode the skateboard up and down the driveway, thinking. She felt more determined than ever to fix things for Mr. Duffy. She had promised Rose that she would come up with plan B, but so far, she hadn't.

How could she convince Mr. Duffy that he needed a dog and Henry needed a home?

She had been so certain she could do it, but now it seemed harder than she thought it would be.

Maybe Mr. Duffy's heart really was a thumping gizzard after all.

HENRY

When Henry got out of the fenced yard, he had run as far away from Wonderland as he could get.

He had run up dirt roads and through fields. He darted across a busy highway and raced through a trailer park. He hurried across parking lots and dashed into some woods behind a shopping center.

Then he had trotted deeper and deeper into the woods, jumping over moss-covered logs and clusters of bramble bushes and wild strawberries. Squirrels scurried out of his way, and birds fluttered wildly out of the trees as he passed.

When he was far enough into the woods, he had stopped, panting.

Then he slept a long, deep sleep.

For two more days, Henry ran along roads and darted

among trees. He crossed fields and jumped across gullies. He followed paths and wandered along the side of narrow, twisting lanes.

He ate berries and bugs and even a tiny frog. Once he had been lucky enough to find a discarded bag on the side of the road with half a cheese sandwich and an apple core. He even turned over a garbage can here and there, gobbling up moldy bread, some fried chicken skin, and a few pieces of doughnuts. He licked tuna clinging to the sides of a slightly rusted can and gnawed on a moldy pork chop bone. When he had come upon a narrow creek winding through the woods, he drank and drank and drank, the cool water tasting finer than any he had ever had before.

Now he lay down under the trees, where the ground was soft with pine needles and rotting leaves, and fell asleep.

He slept until the hooting of an owl and the croaking of frogs woke him up.

It was dark.

The darkest dark that Henry had ever known.

Every now and then, fireflies twinkled in the distance.

Henry felt lonely and scared and hungry.

Maybe he had made a mistake.

Maybe he should go back to Wonderland.

MAVIS

Rose and Mavis sat on the log in the vacant lot, talking about plan B.

Well, actually, it was Rose who was *trying* to talk about plan B.

"So," Rose said, "what's plan B?"

"I'm not sure yet," Mavis said.

"But I thought you were good at coming up with plan B."

"I am."

"Oh." Rose wiped red dirt off her shorts. "I just thought you would've come up with it by now."

"It takes *time* to think up a good plan B." Mavis was starting to feel a little annoyed.

Then Rose didn't say anything, and Mavis started to feel a *lot* annoyed.

"Maybe you can come up with plan B," she said. "I'm the one that's been doing all the thinking."

"But I'm not the one who said I was good at coming up with plan B," Rose said.

Well, didn't that beat all?

Here Mavis had been trying so hard to fix things for Rose and Mr. Duffy. "I've been trying to be a good best friend," she said, kicking at a cluster of Queen Anne's lace beside the log. "If you'd rather have a *different* best friend, go ahead. Maybe one of those girls from the swim team and y'all can be in the mother-daughter book club together."

Then Mavis sat there in steamy silence with her arms crossed and her lips clamped tight.

A dragonfly flitted among the wildflowers in front of them. Mavis kicked at the flowers, making the dragonfly dart away and disappear across the vacant lot.

Finally, Rose broke the silence. "I wouldn't rather have a different best friend," she said.

Mavis kept her arms crossed and her lips clamped tight.

Silence.

Silence.

Silence.

Then Rose said, "Aren't you worried about Mr. Duffy?"

Mavis shrugged. "I guess."

"What do you mean?"

"I mean, yes. Yes, I'm worried about him because I know *you're* worried about him."

And then, quite unexpectedly, that old snake, Mr. Jealousy, showed up and made Mavis say, "All you and Mr. Duffy care about is each other. What about me? Doesn't anybody care about me?"

Uh-oh. Mavis hadn't meant to say that. But it was too late. Rose's face turned a little red, and she said, "Why are you being so mean?"

Then the next thing you know, Rose and Mavis were arguing.

Mavis reminded Rose that she was the one coming up with the ideas to fix things with Mr. Duffy.

Rose pointed out that she had broken every rule in the Tully Rule Book to go along with all of Mavis's crazy ideas.

Mavis said Rose should be glad to have such a fun thing to do as going to Wonderland.

Rose said she thought maybe they were being too hasty trying to get a dog for Mr. Duffy, especially when he didn't even want one.

On and on.

Back and forth.

Until finally Mavis stood up and said, "Fine."

Rose stayed sitting on the log and said, "Fine."

And that was that.

ROSE

The next day, Rose moped.

She rearranged her china horses.

She counted her dresses to see if Mavis had been right.

Yep. Seventeen.

Then she went into Grace's room and wandered around, touching her things and looking at her scrapbook filled with movie ticket stubs and dance recital programs and a lock of hair from a boyfriend.

She went downstairs and stepped on every single square of the marble tile in the foyer.

She sat on the velvet couch in the living room and listened to her mother explaining to Miss Jeeter what to do about the white water ring on the mahogany dining room table. When her mother said something like "That's what coasters are for," Miss Jeeter said something back in a snappy voice.

When Monroe Tucker started the hedge clippers out in the yard, Rose went on the porch and sat between Pete and Larry and watched him trim the boxwoods along the driveway.

But after a very short while, Rose got tired of moping. She thought about getting her skateboard out of the garage and riding it around Magnolia Estates. Wouldn't that surprise everyone?

But, no, that didn't sound like much fun, so Rose decided to visit Mr. Duffy.

Imagine her surprise when she got to the gatehouse and there was Mavis, playing checkers with Mr. Duffy.

In fact, she was so surprised that all she said was, "Oh."

Mr. Duffy said, "Hey, there," and Mavis lifted a limp hand in a half-hearted wave.

"You're playing checkers," Rose said.

Mr. Duffy nodded. "That we are."

"I thought you didn't like playing checkers anymore," Rose said, trying very hard not to sound like a baby, even though she was pretty sure she did.

Mr. Duffy chuckled. "Well, ole Mavis here is one

stubborn mule. I had about as much chance as a grass-hopper in a chicken house trying to say no to her."

"Oh," Rose said again. She was pretty sure Mavis was trying not to smile. She saw the corners of her mouth twitching.

Then suddenly Mavis jumped Mr. Duffy's checkers with three loud slaps on the board and hollered, "Boom! Boom! Boom! King me!"

She jumped off her stool and did a little jig of a dance, pumping her fist and saying, "*That's* what I'm talking about."

Mr. Duffy laughed.

Hard.

Then he took a handkerchief out of his pocket and wiped his eyes.

Jealousy bubbled up inside Rose, making her stomach hurt and her face burn. Then the bubbling jealousy worked its way down to her feet, making her run out the gatehouse door and all the way home.

HENRY

Henry didn't know how many days it had been since he had crawled under that fence and run away from Wonderland.

But each day seemed to get harder.

He wandered through woods during the day, sometimes napping on damp moss in the cool shade of the sycamore trees. At night he searched for food in alleys behind the diners and markets of Landry. Once in a while he wandered through neighborhoods, sniffing around garbage cans and occasionally coming upon a bowl of food left out for somebody's wandering cat.

But Henry wasn't just hungry.

He was lonely.

At least at Wonderland there were other dogs to keep him company.

He used to hate staying cooped up in a kennel so much, but now that he was free, that kennel didn't seem so bad.

And although he'd never had one person to call his own, there had been trainers and handlers around most of the time. And then there was that bald man named Roger who called him "naughty Rocket Boy" and gave him a pat on the head once in a while.

But now that Henry was out of Wonderland, he realized that what he really longed for was someone all his own.

He often thought about those girls.

The wild-haired one and the quiet one.

How they had called him Henry and stroked his sides and kissed his nose.

As the sun began to sink and the fireflies twinkled among the ferns and mayapples scattered through the woods, Henry scratched at the leaves and pine needles to make a soft bed for the night. By the time darkness had settled, he was dreaming. A peaceful dream of being stroked and kissed and loved by someone all his own.

MAVIS

Mavis wasn't a moper.

Mavis was a doer.

A problem solver.

An adventure seeker.

But here she was on a sunny summer day in Landry, Alabama, sitting on a log in a vacant lot, moping.

Because here she was without a best friend again.

She had thought this time would be different.

She had been certain that she and Rose would be real best friends.

Not that fake kind like she'd had before.

The kind where someone *claimed* to be your best friend, and then the next thing you knew, they were telling lies about you on the playground or not saving you a seat on the bus or flinging peas at you in the cafeteria while the other kids at the table laughed.

But now here she was on this log by herself, and Rose was in her fancy house, probably admiring her seventeen dresses or eating tomato aspic on a china plate. Or maybe she was at the mother-daughter book club with a new best friend.

Mavis kept watching the street, hoping to see Rose headed this way.

But she didn't.

The street was empty.

The vacant lot was empty except for the grasshoppers popping up every now and then in the tall, dry weeds.

The sun beat down, burning the back of Mavis's neck and making the red dirt beneath her bare feet warm as toast.

Suddenly Mavis was struck with a feeling.

Loneliness.

A deep, sad loneliness that caught her off guard and made her cry.

A slow, quiet cry.

The tears rolling down her cheeks and dropping onto the dry dirt beside the log.

Mavis thought about that day when Mr. Duffy had talked about Edna keeping the coffee warm and how she had felt so jealous seeing what good friends Rose and Mr. Duffy were.

She thought about Rose going to Wonderland even when she didn't really want to. She thought about how she had gone into the woods where she wasn't supposed to go. How she had borrowed Amanda's bike and gotten her sandals dirty and let Mavis take her mother's quiches and liver pâté.

Mavis wished Rose were here, being her best friend again.

She swished a stick around in the dry dirt beside the log.

She wrote *Rose + Mavis*.

Then she tossed the stick into the bushes and headed home to listen to her mother complain about Mrs. Tully.

ROSE

Rose was pretty sure that she was the unhappiest girl in Landry, Alabama. She sat on Grace's window seat and made a mental list of the reasons she was so unhappy.

1. Mr. Duffy, who had always been so fun and cheerful, was now sad and a little grumpy.
2. That same friend, Mr. Duffy, was getting more and more forgetful and making so many mistakes that folks in Magnolia Estates were getting more and more impatient with him.
3. She had argued with her new (and only) best friend, Mavis, and now they weren't even talking anymore.

4. Mr. Duffy never seemed to want to play checkers with her, but then there he was, playing checkers with Mavis. So now maybe he liked Mavis more than he liked her. But then, who could blame him? Mavis was fun and adventurous and brave, which she, Rose Tully, was not.

5. That poor, sweet dog, Henry, needed a home. And Mavis was so sure that she could convince Mr. Duffy to adopt him, but Rose wasn't so sure.

6. Her mother complained about Miss Jeeter nearly every minute of every day.

7. Her sister, Grace, was gone and Rose needed her.

Seven reasons to be unhappy.

That was a lot.

Suddenly a noise outside made Rose stop thinking about how unhappy she was.

The sound of a skateboard on the driveway.

Mavis.

It had to be Mavis.

Rose jumped up off Grace's window seat and ran

downstairs and out the back door. She hurried through the hydrangea garden to the front of the house.

Sure enough, there was Mavis riding the skateboard up and down the driveway. She glanced over briefly, but then looked away and began to whistle as she rode the skateboard up one side and down the other. Wasn't that just so like Mavis, breaking that rule about not riding the skateboard on the driveway? And then whistling while she did it! Such a Mavis thing to do.

Rose marched out into the middle of the yard with her head high and her arms swinging. Then she took off her sandals and flung them into the air so high that one of them landed in the top of her mother's favorite magnolia tree.

Then she, Rose Tully, scampered around in circles on the grass, not caring one little bit if she got ringworm.

Mavis had stopped riding the skateboard and was standing gape-mouthed at the edge of the yard, staring up at Rose's sandal in the magnolia tree. Then she grinned at Rose and hollered, "*That's* what I'm talking about!"

Rose grinned back.

Then the two of them headed up the street toward the gatehouse, Mavis's skateboard whirring and Rose's bare feet slap, slap, slapping on the asphalt road.

MAVIS

Mavis could hardly believe her eyes when Rose had flung her sandals up in the air like that. So unlike her. And then she'd gone and run around the yard barefoot as if she'd never even *heard* the word *ringworm*.

This was a new Rose.

And best of all, a Rose who wasn't mad at her anymore.

Mavis was relieved.

Now they could get back to being best friends again.

When they reached the gatehouse, Mavis hopped off the skateboard and said, "Okay, here's plan B. We'll do the ole guilt trip."

Rose looked puzzled. "What guilt trip?"

"You know, like, make Mr. Duffy think his heart

really *is* a thumping gizzard if he can go and let a poor, innocent dog have no home of his own and nobody to love him."

"I don't know," Rose said. "That seems kind of mean."

"No, it's not," Mavis said. "I'm really good at guilt-tripping."

When they got inside the gatehouse, Mr. Duffy was on the phone telling somebody he was certain he had never had the names Joleen and Travis Bivens on the guest list. Then he held the phone away from his ear and rolled his eyes.

The person on the other end of the phone was mad. Mavis could hear snatches of loud, angry words.

"I *told* you—"

"How many times—"

"—so embarrassing—"

Mr. Duffy shook his head and winked at Rose and Mavis. Then he put the phone back to his ear and said, "Yes, ma'am," and hung up.

"You don't have to hang from a tree to be a nut," he said. "And that woman is most definitely a nut. I swear she could start an argument with an empty room."

Then he turned to Rose and said, "Rose Tully! What

got into you, running out of here like you done the other day? You trying to make an old man older?"

Rose blushed. "No, sir."

Mavis jumped in quick before the old worried Rose came back and took over the new brave Rose.

"Everything's good now. Right, Rose?" she said.

Rose nodded.

"We want to talk to you about Henry," Mavis said.

Before Mr. Duffy had a chance to say anything, Mavis started working on the guilt trip. She told Mr. Duffy how Henry was all alone in this world. How he'd devoted his whole life to racing, and now he was a has-been and nobody wanted him. How all he wanted was a little love and a home of his own. Was that so wrong?

On and on.

Guilt-tripping like crazy.

A couple of times Mr. Duffy opened his mouth to say something, but Mavis kept right on going. Every now and then she said, "Right, Rose?" but she didn't stop long enough for Rose to do more than nod.

When she finally felt like that guilt trip was the best that it could be, Mavis stopped.

Mr. Duffy took his cap off, ran his hand over his bald

head, and put it back on again. He looked out the window and up at the ceiling and down at the floor.

Then he took a breath and opened his mouth to speak,
but a noise at the screen door made him stop.

He looked at the door.

Rose looked at the door.

Mavis looked at the door.

There, scratching on the screen, was Henry.

HENRY

When Henry had wakened from that dream about having someone all his own, he'd made a decision.

He was tired of being alone in the woods.

He was going to look for those girls.

They had been so nice to him, kissing him and petting him.

So he ran for hours through fields, across roads, and in and out of woods until he found what he was looking for.

The wrought-iron fence where the freckled girl had left him bowls of food.

He sniffed around the ferns and leaves and wild raspberries. He wandered in and out of the fragrant pines and shady sycamores.

But those girls were not there.

Then he remembered the little house where they had taken him. The one with the gray-haired man.

But he also remembered that that was where Roger had come to get him.

What if Roger came again?

But maybe this time something good would happen.

Maybe this time Roger wouldn't come.

Maybe this time those girls would let him stay with them.

Henry had followed the same route as before, running along the fence and up the asphalt street to the little house beside the gate.

His heart had leaped with joy when he heard voices through the screen door.

Voices of those girls and the gray-haired man.

He scratched on the screen.

When they saw him, the girls squealed, "Henry!" They ran to the door and let him in and showered him with hugs and kisses.

Henry had never been showered with hugs and kisses before.

The old man said, "Jeekers! How in the heck did that dog get back here?"

"Please don't call Wonderland," the wild-haired girl said.

Then she put her hands together like she was praying and added, "Let's keep him for a little while."

The quiet girl said, "He's so skinny! I bet he's hungry."

The old man heaved a big sigh and shuffled over to his desk. He took a paper bag out of a drawer and brought Henry a tuna fish sandwich.

Henry had never had a tuna fish sandwich before.

He gobbled it up, and then he put his head in the old man's lap.

The old man put his hand on top of Henry's head.

His hand was warm.

Henry let out a little whine of contentment and wagged his tail to say *thank you*.

ROSE

Rose looked at Mr. Duffy sitting there with his hand on Henry's head, and for the first time she had a little glimmer of hope that maybe, just maybe, Mavis's plan had worked.

Maybe all that great guilt-tripping had convinced Mr. Duffy to keep Henry.

But that glimmer disappeared when Mr. Duffy said, "Y'all know this dog has to go back where he belongs, don't you?"

And then, of course, Mavis had jumped in, the way Mavis always jumped in, reminding Mr. Duffy that Henry was up for adoption and needed a home.

Rose was afraid Mr. Duffy was going to start talking

about how he was too old to get another dog, but that didn't happen.

Instead, Henry lifted his head off Mr. Duffy's lap and walked over to Queenie's bed and lay down.

The little gatehouse grew quiet while Rose and Mavis and Mr. Duffy looked at Henry curled up on Queenie's bed, already fast asleep.

He looked so peaceful there on the fluffy round bed with QUEENIE embroidered in blue.

Rose's mind raced.

Would Mr. Duffy get mad at Henry for sleeping in Queenie's bed?

Would he wake him up and tell him to get off that bed? It wasn't his bed.

But Mr. Duffy didn't do that.

What he did do was look at Rose and Mavis and say, "I've got to call Wonderland to come get that dog."

MAVIS

Mavis dropped onto the stool with a big, heaving sigh.

She made a pouty face.

She let out another big, heaving sigh.

But it was no use.

Mr. Duffy called Wonderland to come get Henry.

Mavis went over to where Henry was still sleeping on Queenie's bed and lay on the floor beside him, trying her best to look pitiful.

She was glad to see that Rose was doing a pretty good job of looking pitiful, too. She sat slumped in Mr. Duffy's desk chair, spinning it slowly in circles with her toe.

Mr. Duffy stood at the gatehouse door, watching for the van from Wonderland.

It didn't take long for the van to arrive and Roger to come into the gatehouse carrying a leash.

"I swanee, Rocket Boy," he said. "What are we going to do about you?"

At the sound of Roger's voice, Henry opened his eyes and sat up.

Mavis threw her arms around him and hugged his neck. Then she turned her pitiful face to Roger and asked, "What's going to happen to him?"

"He's gotta go back to Wonderland," Roger said. "I'm trying to find a foster home for him, but no luck yet."

Mavis forgot about making her pitiful face and jumped up off the floor.

"Foster home!" she said. "Really?"

"Sure," Roger said. "We always try to find foster homes for our rescue pups. It's better for them to be in a home instead of cooped up in that adoption center."

Mavis whipped her head around to look at Mr. Duffy. "Did you hear that?" she said.

Mr. Duffy held up a hand and said, "Hold on now, missy, I don't—"

"But it's perfect!" Mavis said. "Right, Rose?"

Rose looked at Henry and then at Mr. Duffy and said, "Yes! It's perfect!"

Mavis grinned. Finally Rose wasn't being wishy-washy and hemming and hawing like she usually did. Now it was time to try the old guilt trip again.

"You won't be *keeping* him," Mavis said. "You'll be giving him a nice place to live until somebody whose heart isn't a thumping gizzard comes along to help a sad, homeless dog."

Mr. Duffy frowned. "Don't be pulling that on me, Miss Mavis."

Mavis tried to look innocent. "Pulling what on you?"

Mr. Duffy cocked his head at her and narrowed his eyes.

"Just think what good company Henry would be," Rose said. "I bet he'd like to go fishing with you down at the lake and—"

"Now don't y'all go ganging up on me," Mr. Duffy said. He stroked his chin and looked down at Henry.

"See how quiet he is?" Mavis said. "He hasn't barked one single time since we found him."

"And I bet he'd love your trailer," Rose said. "And he could ride in the truck with you and stay here in the gatehouse with you while you work."

On and on they went.

Mavis, then Rose, then Mavis again.

Working on Mr. Duffy until he finally turned to Roger and said, "So, tell me what I'd have to do to foster this dog."

Roger told Mr. Duffy about filling out some paperwork and having a home inspection to make sure Alabama Rocket Boy would be safe.

"Then just take him home, feed him, and love on him a little," Roger said, "until I find someone to adopt him."

Mr. Duffy looked down at Henry. "So, it's only temporary, right?"

"Right."

"And I can take him back to Wonderland if it don't work out, right?"

"Right."

Mr. Duffy scratched his chin. "Well, I reckon I can take him for a little while."

Mavis let out a whoop, and she and Rose did their special handshake.

Slapping, snapping, and fist-bumping.

Plan B had worked out pretty good.

Now all they had to do was make sure that Mr. Duffy fell in love with Henry. And she had no doubt that she and Rose would be really good at that.

ROSE

Rose sat between Pete and Larry, feeling lighter. All those things that had been weighing her down were beginning to lift.

She was feeling braver every day. Just yesterday she had gone barefoot and ridden her skateboard around Magnolia Estates. Even in front of the Simms' house with Amanda and a bunch of girls doing gymnastics on the lawn. She had even waved to them. Amanda had looked surprised, but she had waved back.

Then she had told her mother she wasn't interested in joining the mother-daughter book club if Mavis and her mother couldn't join, too.

But the biggest weight had been worrying about Mr. Duffy. Now he was taking care of Henry, and she could already tell he was happier. He whistled while he worked in the gatehouse. He'd started saying "What's shakin', bacon?" like he used to. When it was time to go home, he said, "Look out, catfish, here I come." He had even played the kazoo yesterday. Things were definitely getting better.

But Rose did have one little twinge of worry. Her mother and the ladies in her bridge club were still complaining about Mr. Duffy. He forgot to call someone to check on the floodlights down by the tennis courts. He let a car full of teenagers come through the gate to visit Tyler Reed, and they were definitely not on the approved visitor list. And Audrey Jonker was almost certain Mr. Duffy had been sleeping when she drove through the gate the other day.

Rose pushed that worry away and skipped up the street to the gatehouse. She wished Mavis were home, but today was Miss Jeeter's day off and the two of them had taken the bus to town.

As soon as she went into the gatehouse, Mr. Duffy said, "Hey there, Rose Petal!"

Henry lay on Queenie's bed beside Mr. Duffy's chair, thumping his tail on the floor. Rose noticed some of Queenie's old toys on the bed beside him.

Even that felt monkey with the stuffing ripped out of it. Queenie's favorite.

Rose couldn't help but smile about that.

Everything was feeling so good again. Maybe Mr. Duffy would do some magic tricks or ask her to tap dance.

But just when Rose was thinking Mr. Duffy might take out his kazoo, he put his hands on her shoulders and said, "I have something to tell you, Rose."

HENRY

Henry had never known that dogs could live a life like the one he was living with Mr. Duffy.

Ever since the day that Roger had gotten into the Wonderland van and driven away from the little gatehouse without him, Henry's life had been full of firsts.

He had ridden in a truck with his head out the window, letting the wind blow his flapping ears, and watching a whole world of stores and houses and fields and barns whiz by.

He had walked beside Mr. Duffy around a lake, the water glistening in the late-afternoon sun.

He had gone inside Mr. Duffy's trailer, which smelled like he imagined a home would smell. Like old shoes, biscuits, and bacon.

Mr. Duffy made hot dogs and baked beans for supper and shared them with him, even letting him up on the couch to eat from a paper plate beside him.

Sometimes Mr. Duffy was quiet, but sometimes he talked to Henry. He grumbled about his arthritis and remarked about the evening air getting a little cooler and apologized for his lousy cooking.

The scent of another dog lingered on the sofa and the rugs and even on Mr. Duffy's slippers under the bed. Henry wondered where that dog was now.

When the sun went down on that first night, Mr. Duffy turned out the lights in the trailer and motioned for Henry to sleep on the rug beside his bed. In the middle of the night Henry jumped onto the bed and nestled down among the cool, thin sheets. When Mr. Duffy woke the next morning to find him there, he mumbled something under his breath, but he didn't make him get down. Henry slept on the bed every night after that.

In the mornings, they ate scrambled eggs and bacon for breakfast and went for a walk down by the lake. Then they got in the truck and drove to the little gatehouse where Rose and Mavis came to visit every day.

But today Rose had come alone.

Henry was glad to see her and thumped his tail to let her know.

Then Mr. Duffy had gotten a serious look on his face and told Rose something that made her cry.

MAVIS

Mavis stared out the window of the bus at the sights of Landry, Alabama, beyond the gates of Magnolia Estates. The trailer parks with dirt-stained trailers sitting every which way among the white oak trees. The cotton fields stretched out between farmhouses with sheets on the clotheslines and pickup trucks filled with bales of hay in the gravel driveways. Sometimes children waved to the bus from their front porches.

The sickly sweet smell of her mother's cologne drifted toward Mavis, making her eyes water. She waved her hand in front of her nose and opened the window of the bus, letting the hot summer air blow in.

"Tell me again why I had to come with you," Mavis said.

"I want you to see more of Landry, May May."

"Why?"

" 'Cause I think you'll like it. There's a lot more to Landry than that snooty Magnolia Estates, you know."

But Mavis knew there was some other reason for this bus trip. That tightness in her stomach told her this wasn't a sightseeing trip. She was almost eleven years old. Did her mother think she was still that little six-year-old Mavis who believed everything her mother told her? The Mavis who went along on every new adventure with her mother, thinking everything was going to turn out great, like her mother promised it would?

Well, she wasn't that little Mavis anymore. *This* Mavis could smell something fishy a mile away. And in addition to that sickly sweet smell of her mother's cologne, there was most definitely a fishy smell wafting around Mavis as she sat on that bus.

Before long, the view outside the window began to change. The farms and cotton fields disappeared, and in their place were neighborhoods with tree-lined streets and kids playing in the yards. As they got closer to town, they passed JBJ's Used Car Lot, Bucky's Diner, Oak Grove Baptist Church, Ruth Ann's Cut 'n' Curl.

"Check it out!" Her mother leaned over and pointed out the window. "That's your school."

Landry Elementary School was a two-story brick building beside a dusty playground and a tiny square of blacktop with a basketball hoop. Scattered in the dirt and gravel were remnants of long-ago recesses. Half of a frayed jump rope. A deflated soccer ball.

Finally the bus came to a stop, brakes screeching.

"This is it!" her mother said. "Come on!"

Mavis followed her mother up the aisle and down the steps to the sidewalk. The doors of the bus closed with a whoosh, and the bus drove off, leaving a puff of black smoke behind it.

"Ta-da!" Her mother threw her arms out and grinned at Mavis.

There in front of them were four small apartment buildings. Two on each side of a wide strip of dry, yellowing grass. In the grass strip were a couple of picnic tables and a swing set. Kids played on the swings while grown-ups sat at the picnic tables, playing cards and bouncing babies on their laps.

Some of the apartments on the ground floor had pots of flowers by their doors or bicycles lying beside the walkway. The second-floor apartments had tiny balconies where laundry dried on the railings and old people sat in aluminum lawn chairs.

A sun-bleached, peeling sign out by the road read GARDEN VIEW APARTMENTS.

"Where's the garden?" Mavis asked.

Her mother frowned. "What?"

"The garden." Mavis nodded toward the sign, making a clump of curls flop over her forehead.

"Aw, come on, May May," her mother said. "Can't you look on the bright side of things for once?"

"Which side is the bright one?" Mavis was trying very hard to act nonchalant, but her insides were stirring around like a swarm of angry bees, and that fishy smell was getting stinkier by the minute.

"They've got a couple of empty apartments and I'm telling you, May, they're really nice inside." Her mother gave her a little poke on the arm. "Dishwashers and everything," she added.

Mavis didn't want her mother to beat around the bush. She wanted her to go straight to the cold, hard facts.

"Why are we here?" she asked.

Her mother shifted her purse from one shoulder to

the other. "Okay. I'm thinking of getting me a new job in Landry. A better job. A job where some highfalutin woman doesn't make me feel like a dumb, worthless piece of nothing."

"And what job is that?"

Her mother flopped down on the bus stop bench.

"I don't know yet," she said. "But I've made some calls, and I've got a couple of prospects. I got a good feeling about this, May May."

Mavis's swarming-bee insides turned into one big ball of dread.

Her mother had had a good feeling about a lot of things before. But most of the time, those things had turned out to be a long way from good.

ROSE

"I'm quitting, Rose Petal," Mr. Duffy said.

"Quitting?"

Mr. Duffy nodded.

"This job?" Rose asked.

He nodded again.

Then all the worry that had been swirling around Rose for so long came crashing down.

Boom!

She sat in Mr. Duffy's desk chair and sobbed.

Mr. Duffy put his hands on the arm of the chair and said, "Don't cry, Rosie. It's not the end of the world."

But it felt like the end of the world to Rose.

At least, the end of *her* world. She couldn't imagine Magnolia Estates without Mr. Duffy.

"Aw, now, you don't need to be hanging around an old whomper-jawed geezer like me," he said. "You got yourself a fine new friend in Mavis."

But Rose kept sobbing, taking big gulps of air and swiping at her tearstained face.

Mr. Duffy continued in a soft voice.

He was too old for this job, he said.

He had outlived his usefulness with this job, he told her.

He might as well get out while the gettin' was good, he explained.

"I never really did feel like the folks behind this gate took a shine to me," he said. "I reckon I've always felt like I was hanging around like a hair in a biscuit. You know, not fitting in with these uppity folks." Then he gave Rose's shoulders a little shake. "Not that your folks are uppity, Rosie. They raised a fine girl like you, so that means something in my book."

Rose's head was spinning, and her heart was breaking.

The day had come.

Mr. Duffy was leaving.

"But wait'll you hear the good part," he said, giving her knee a little poke.

Rose wiped her nose and looked at him through teary eyes. "What good part?"

"The part about my *new* job," he said.

"What new job?"

"At Wonderland!"

"Wonderland?"

Mr. Duffy nodded. "Wonderland."

Then he went on to explain that Wonderland was closing and that the bald man, Roger, needed help finding homes for all the greyhounds there.

"We're gonna be busier than a moth in a mitten," he said.

"But why is Wonderland closing?" Rose asked.

"Well, you know, dog racing just ain't that popular anymore," Mr. Duffy said. "A lot of folks think those dogs don't have such a good life, cooped up in kennels half the dang day. Spraining their knees and working so hard."

He glanced over at Henry, asleep on Queenie's bed beside the desk. "Dogs need homes with folks who love 'em and give 'em tuna fish sandwiches once in a while. They need to sleep on a couch and have room to run free and chase real rabbits instead of fake ones around in circles on that dang racetrack."

He gazed out the window and nodded. "This is a good thing for those dogs." Turning back to Rose, he added, "And the job's only two days a week. Just think about all the fishing time me and Henry are gonna have."

"You and Henry?"

"Well, yeah, you know, till I find somebody to adopt him," Mr. Duffy said. "*And* I'll be able to make sure he gets a good home."

"But what if you don't like that job?" Rose said. "Will you come back?"

Mr. Duffy leaned down and took Rose's chin in his hand. It was warm and smelled faintly of fish. "The corn's off the cob, Rosie. Too late to come back."

Then the two of them sat for a while, not talking.

Just listening to Henry snore, until Rose said, "I better go."

MAVIS

Mavis sat on the log in the vacant lot and stared glumly at the wildflowers and the bramble bushes and the small gold sign that read BUILD YOUR DREAM HOME HERE.

Dream home.

Ha!

Mavis had never had a dream home in her life.

Her mother had always made her *think* that each new place they landed in was their dream home.

The condo in Atlanta.

The apartment over the Chinese restaurant in South Carolina.

That shabby old house they shared with that crazy lady someplace Mavis couldn't even remember.

That brick house owned by her mother's hotheaded boyfriend in Hadley, Georgia.

On and on and on.

Dream homes?

Hardly.

And every single time, Mavis had tried to have a best friend. But every single time, they hadn't stayed long enough for that to happen.

Now, finally, they had a nice place here in Landry, Alabama, and she really *did* have a best friend.

Mavis felt sure that if her mother quit her job with the Tullys, Rose wouldn't want to be her best friend anymore.

Why would she?

They wouldn't be able to see each other every day.

They couldn't have any more adventures like the one they'd had when they went to Wonderland.

They couldn't visit Mr. Duffy and play checkers.

Besides, Mrs. Tully would be so mad at her mother for quitting, she wouldn't want Rose to play with Mavis, anyway.

Then a thought popped into Mavis's head.

School would be starting in a few weeks.

They would see each other at school!

They could still be best friends.

They could eat lunch together and have club meetings at recess and choose each other as partners in science class and stuff like that.

But then another thought popped into Mavis's head.

Did Rose even go to Landry Elementary School?

Probably not.

She probably went to some fancy school where the kids wore uniforms and went on field trips to Disney World and the lunch ladies served them fried chicken and apple pie on china plates.

Mavis had been avoiding Rose the last few days, staying up in the apartment or dashing down here to the vacant lot. Not even going to see Mr. Duffy in case Rose was there. But now she looked at the empty spot on the log beside her and felt that loneliness come creeping back.

She needed to see Rose.

Mavis made her way up the street, her thoughts weighing her down and making her walk slow and slump-shouldered. Unfortunately, walking up the street toward her was Amanda Simm, wearing a bathing suit and carrying a towel.

Dang!

Mavis was not in the mood to talk to *her.*

"Hey," Amanda called when she saw Mavis.

Mavis said, "Hey," and tried to keep walking, but Amanda stopped beside her and said, "So, I guess I was right about Mr. Duffy."

"What do you mean?"

"About him leaving."

"Leaving?"

Amanda nodded and flicked her cantaloupe-colored ponytail over her shoulder.

"Where's he going?" Mavis asked.

"I don't know."

"How do you know he's leaving?"

"My mother told me," Amanda said. "Is he keeping that dog y'all took up there?"

"Yes." Mavis's fib came out fast and easy. But if her plan worked, and she was sure it would, Mr. Duffy *was* going to keep Henry.

Now her thoughts were racing. Did Rose know about Mr. Duffy? If she did, she would be really upset. Mavis suddenly had guilt poking at her from every direction. She had been so busy moping about her mother's new job that she hadn't even thought much about Rose. A best friend wouldn't do that. *Why* was she so bad at being a best friend?

"What's Rose going to do?" Amanda asked.

"What do you mean?"

"All she ever does is stay up at the gatehouse with Mr. Duffy," Amanda said. "There's lots of other stuff to do in Magnolia Estates. The Junior Garden Club, the mother-daughter book club, the tennis team, the—"

"Rose doesn't want to do any of that stuff," Mavis said.

"She could do gymnastics in my yard with me and Mimi Fay," Amanda said. "You can come, too. Unless y'all would rather play with those lions on Rose's porch."

Mavis's face burned with anger. She wanted to give that cantaloupe ponytail a good yank. But for once, self-control tapped her on the shoulder and told her to cool it.

Then she stood up straight and lifted her chin and walked away from Amanda Simm. She needed to check on her best friend, Rose.

HENRY

Henry didn't know what Mr. Duffy had said that had made Rose cry, but things hadn't been quite the same since.

Rose didn't come to visit as often, and when she did, she seemed a little sad.

And Mavis hadn't come to the gatehouse at all.

And Mr. Duffy just wasn't himself.

For one thing, he'd stopped whistling.

He used to whistle while he made hot dogs for supper.

He whistled when he gathered his fishing gear and headed for the lake, calling for Henry to come with him.

And he whistled when he tidied up the trailer, putting his old leather slippers neatly under the bed, taking wet towels out to the clothesline to dry, and washing the plastic bowl that Henry ate out of beside the kitchen table.

Lucky for Henry, Mr. Duffy still tore off pieces of his hot dog and tossed them into the bowl, but things didn't feel the same as they had a few days ago. Henry was pretty sure it had to do with whatever Mr. Duffy had told Rose that made her cry.

So when Mr. Duffy went for walks down by the lake, his head down and his hands clasped behind his back, Henry made sure he stayed right beside him.

And when Mr. Duffy sat on the lumpy couch and watched TV until he fell asleep, Henry lay at his feet, resting his head on Mr. Duffy's slipper.

And when Mr. Duffy woke up in front of the TV and ambled off to bed, Henry followed along and settled in among the sheets next to him, waiting until he heard Mr. Duffy's snoring before he allowed himself to drift off.

Some nights, while he waited for Mr. Duffy to snore, Henry thought about this new life he was living.

He had never slept in the glow of a television before.

He had never snuggled in the sheets of a person's bed before.

He had never even eaten a tuna fish sandwich before.

This life sure was different from his life at Wonderland.

More than anything, he hoped he could stay here with Mr. Duffy in the little trailer by the lake.

ROSE

Rose stabbed a few grains of wild rice and nibbled on them. Then she mashed her fork into her spinach soufflé and waited for her mother to say, "Stop playing with your food, Rose."

But instead, her mother said, "Miss Jeeter has given her notice, Robert."

Rose's stomach did a somersault. She froze with her fork in the air, looking down at the spinach soufflé. She wanted to cover her ears so she wouldn't have to hear what came next, but she stayed there frozen like that.

Her father raised his eyebrows. "Oh?"

"She's found another job," her mother said.

"I guess that's just as well," her father said.

"What's that supposed to mean?"

Then they argued for a few minutes.

Rose's father saying how her mother had never seemed happy with Miss Jeeter, and her mother saying, "Well, do you blame me, Robert?" Then she asked what she was supposed to do now. She couldn't be expected to have no help.

When there seemed to be a lull in the conversation, Rose asked, "What's her new job?"

Her mother looked surprised to see that Rose was still sitting there. "Receptionist at Clyde Waterman's insurance agency." She glanced over at Rose's father, who kept quiet, then she added under her breath, "That ought to be good."

"Will she and Mavis stay in the apartment over the garage?" Rose asked.

Her mother sat up straighter, her back pressed against the mahogany chair. "Of course not!" she said.

Rose set her fork down. "May I be excused?"

Her mother opened her mouth to speak, but before she could, Rose's father said, "You may."

Rose placed her perfectly ironed linen napkin neatly next to her plate and went upstairs to Grace's room.

MAVIS

Mavis rang the "Ode to Joy" doorbell.

Mrs. Tully opened the door and looked surprised to see Mavis.

"Is Rose here?" Mavis asked.

"She is."

"I need to talk to her."

Mrs. Tully lifted an eyebrow and opened the screen door. Mavis fought the urge to hopscotch across the gleaming marble tiles and take the stairs two at a time. Instead, she hurried up to Rose's room, her bare feet sinking into the soft, thick carpet.

But Rose's room was empty.

So Mavis went down to Grace's room, and there was

Rose, sitting on the window seat, hugging her knees and looking pitiful with a capital *P*.

Mavis sat down beside her and said, "I heard about Mr. Duffy."

Rose's chin quivered, and she said, "I heard about your mother's new job."

"And we have to move," Mavis said.

Then she told Rose about Garden View Apartments.

"But we can still be best friends," Mavis said. "We can do everything together at school."

Rose's mouth dropped open a little, and she stared at Mavis. "What school are you going to?" she asked.

Mavis jerked her head in the direction of the highway. "Landry Elementary."

"But I don't go to that school."

Disappointment crashed down on top of Mavis so hard she nearly fell right off the window seat. "You don't?" she said, even though in her heart she had known that all along.

Rose shook her head. Then she explained that she went to a school called Grove Road Academy in the next town over. A lot of kids in Magnolia Estates went there.

"Oh," Mavis said in a voice so tiny she hardly recognized it as her own.

Rose rested her chin on her knees and stared glumly out the window.

"What's that?" Mavis said, pointing to something on the windowsill next to Rose.

"A silver dollar."

Rose told Mavis how Grace had found it on the beach, and it was special.

"She gave it to me when she left for college," Rose said, putting the coin in the palm of her hand and drawing little circles on it with her finger.

Then Rose told Mavis about Mr. Duffy's new job. How he would be helping to find homes for the greyhounds at Wonderland because it was closing.

"Why's it closing?" Mavis asked.

"I guess people don't go to the racetrack as much anymore. And the dogs need to have better lives instead of just racing all the time."

"I know you're going to miss Mr. Duffy," Mavis said. "I will, too."

Rose nodded. "And I'm going to miss you."

"You are?"

Rose nodded again.

Mavis felt a little tingle inside. She was pretty sure no one had ever missed her before. When she'd moved away from all those places, had anybody ever said, "Whatever happened to that girl Mavis? I sure do miss her."

Probably not.

But here was Rose, a real best friend, who was going to miss her when she moved out of the little apartment over the garage.

Then Mavis said something she had never said before. "I'm going to miss you, too."

HENRY

Each day, as soon as the sun came up, Henry and Mr. Duffy headed down to the lake. They strolled through the dewy grass, listening to the birds chirping their good-morning songs and watching the turtles in the lake climb onto logs to bathe in the warm sun.

Sometimes Mr. Duffy threw a stick for Henry to fetch or pointed out a rabbit for him to chase. His hip still hurt him occasionally, but not nearly as much as it had when he was racing.

After breakfast, they were off to the little gatehouse at Magnolia Estates.

The beginning of a new day.

But then one day, something bad happened.

Something that made Henry's heart race.

Instead of driving to Magnolia Estates, Mr. Duffy drove to Wonderland.

What was going on?

Why was Mr. Duffy taking him to Wonderland?

When Henry saw Roger come out to the truck to greet them, he began to shake.

When Mr. Duffy opened the door of the truck and motioned for Henry to follow him into the cinder-block building with dogs howling in their kennels, Henry tucked his tail between his legs and hung his head.

But when they got inside, Mr. Duffy and Roger talked a while, and then Mr. Duffy took an old blanket out of his truck and made a bed for Henry beside a desk.

All morning long, Mr. Duffy looked at papers and talked on the phone. Henry stayed on the blanket, wondering what was going on. Was Mr. Duffy going to leave him here? Just the thought of it made Henry's heart ache.

But then, at the end of the day, when Mr. Duffy motioned for him to get back in the truck, Henry's heart soared.

Mr. Duffy wasn't leaving him at Wonderland after all!

They drove back to the little trailer by the lake, and Henry chased bees and romped in the weeds while Mr. Duffy fished.

Then the two of them had liverwurst on white bread for supper while sitting on the couch in the glow of the television.

When the sun went down and the moon came up, the crickets chirped and the fireflies flickered down by the lake.

And Mr. Duffy and Henry went to bed.

MAVIS

Once again, Mavis found herself whispering goodbye.

Goodbye to the little apartment over the garage.

Goodbye to Pete and Larry.

Goodbye to Magnolia Estates.

Rose and Mavis sat in the back seat of the Tullys' shiny black car on their way to the bus stop, staring glumly out the window.

Summer was over.

School would be starting in a few days.

Mr. Duffy was gone.

And now Rose and Mavis wouldn't be together every day.

Up front, Mrs. Tully sat ramrod straight and gripped the steering wheel while Miss Jeeter complained.

The humidity was ruining her hair.

She had lost her reading glasses again.

Why in the world did cable TV cost so much?

On and on.

As if anyone cared, Mavis thought, glaring at the back of her mother's head.

She was going to hate Garden View Apartments, and she was going to make sure her mother knew it.

She glanced over at Rose, who stared out the window, looking small and pitiful.

When they got to the bus stop, Mavis slammed the car door extra hard, ignoring her mother's look of disapproval.

Rose helped Mavis get the overstuffed duffel bag out of the trunk, and then they looked at each other with sad eyes and droopy shoulders and did their special handshake in gloomy silence.

Slapping, snapping, and fist-bumping.

Miss Jeeter got out of the car, wiggled her fingers at Mrs. Tully, and said, "Toodle-oo," before settling on the bus stop bench with her duct-taped suitcase.

When the bus rumbled into sight, Rose handed Mavis a small white box tied with purple ribbon and quickly climbed into the front seat of the car beside her mother.

As the Tullys' car pulled away, Mavis opened the box. Nestled inside, on a bed of tissue paper, was Grace's silver dollar.

Mavis watched the car disappear around the corner and thought about that day when Mr. Duffy had talked about vines and taters and told Edna to keep the coffee warm. She remembered how jealous she had been of Rose and Mr. Duffy being such good friends. But now Rose had given her this silver dollar that meant so much to her. Maybe she, Mavis Jeeter, had finally learned how to be a good best friend.

Mavis tried her hardest to hate their new apartment, but, actually, it was kind of nice.

It had a microwave and a dishwasher.

She had her own room.

And there was a soda machine down by the laundry room.

Mavis also tried to stay mad at her mother, but it was getting harder every day.

Her mother liked her new job at Clyde Waterman's insurance agency.

She worked from seven to three, so she was home for Mavis after school.

She had a big desk with a fancy computer and a view of the parking lot.

Mr. Waterman loved the way she was so friendly with folks on the phone.

There were some other women who worked there who invited her out to lunch.

And the only thing she ever complained about lately was the bathroom faucet in their new apartment, which dripped all night and kept her awake.

Then one evening, her mother propped her bare feet on the railing of the balcony and said, "I think this might be it, May May. I think Landry, Alabama, is where we'll stay."

Mavis had heard that before, so she pretended to be interested in a caterpillar inching along the top of the railing.

"I *love* this job," her mother said.

Well, that was a first. Her mother had never said *that* before.

"And they're sending me to *school*," her mother went on.

Mavis kept watching that caterpillar and said, "What for?"

"To learn about *insurance*!" her mother said in a

voice so excited you would've thought she'd said they were flying her to Paris to go shopping. "And after that," she added, "I'll get to do more than just answer the phone. So I'm pretty sure I'll make more money."

Her mother took her feet off the railing and said, "And guess what else?"

Mavis waited.

"I bought a car!" her mother squealed.

Mavis jumped up. "Really?"

"Really."

Mavis could hardly believe this stroke of good luck. "Will you take me and Rose to visit Mr. Duffy at Wonderland?"

"Sure I will, May May."

Mavis sat back down and smiled out at the kids playing in the courtyard below. Her mother had never even liked her job before, much less loved it. She had never gone to school before. And she had definitely never bought a car. This seemed like a good sign.

Maybe things were going to work out in Landry after all.

ROSE

At first, when Mavis had called to tell her about her mother's new car, Rose had been excited. Miss Jeeter had offered to drive them to Wonderland to visit Mr. Duffy. But Rose was pretty sure her mother would never let her go. She hadn't told Mavis that, of course. Mavis would tell her not to worry.

Mavis would say, "Trust me."

But still, Rose worried.

When her mother called her to supper, Rose clomped heavily down the stairs, across the marble foyer, and into the dining room.

"The new gatekeeper starts Monday," her mother said.

Her father said, "That's good," and concentrated on the roasted brussels sprouts.

Her mother made a sour face. "I'm so glad that crazy Mr. Duffy is gone, and we don't have to be embarrassed to have guests over anymore."

When Rose heard that, a funny thing happened.

First she felt sad.

Then she felt mad.

And then she felt brave.

She sat up very straight, put her hands in her lap, and said, "Miss Jeeter got a car. She's going to take Mavis and me to Wonderland to visit Mr. Duffy."

There!

She had said it!

Her bravery settled over her, making her lift her chin a little and set a smile on her face.

A small smile, but still . . .

Her mother looked at her as if she had just spoken Greek. Then she looked at Rose's father, whose mouth was turned up in the tiniest trace of a smile.

Then she turned back to Rose and said, "Are you out of your mind?"

"No, ma'am."

Her mother said, "Absolutely not," but her father said, "I don't see what's so wrong with it, Cora." He stabbed a piece of leg of lamb off the platter in front of him and turned to Rose. "Maybe I can drive you to Mavis's after work some time."

Her mother folded her arms and sat back in her chair, tight-lipped and red-faced.

And then Rose's bravery began to grow, making her feel as if it would lift her right up out of her chair and spin her around the chandelier and carry her out of the French doors and into the yard, where she would hover over the potted ferns like a hummingbird. Wouldn't Monroe Tucker be surprised?

With all that bravery spinning around her, Rose explained to her mother that she didn't want to have to do things with Amanda Simm anymore. She told her how Amanda liked going to the mall and talking about lip gloss, but she didn't. She told her that Amanda said mean things sometimes, especially when she was with other girls, but Mavis never did.

"Grace thinks I'm lucky to have a friend like Mavis," Rose said.

Her father nodded. "I agree."

* * *

"I know it's not a *new* new car," Miss Jeeter said as she drove Rose and Mavis to Wonderland, "but it's new to me." She had hung a pair of Mavis's baby booties from the rearview mirror and taped a plastic flower to the radio antenna so she could find the car in the parking lot at the grocery store.

When they got to Wonderland, Mr. Duffy greeted them with, "What's shakin', bacon?"

"Let's play gin rummy," Mavis said, shuffling the cards on Mr. Duffy's desk in the cinder-block building.

Rose and Mavis and Mr. Duffy played cards all afternoon, interrupted every now and then by someone calling about adopting a dog. Henry lay curled up on his blanket bed beside the desk, making little yipping noises as he dreamed a doggie dream.

Suddenly the door opened, and a man with two noisy kids stepped inside. While the kids ran from kennel to kennel, making the dogs bark, the man explained that they were looking for a dog.

it has to be one that's good with kids," the man said. "And won't chase cats."

Mr. Duffy introduced them to one dog after another.

Chuckie.

Caroline.

Gabe.

Pippin.

Henry got up from his blanket bed and went over to greet the kids, wagging his tail and letting them rub his ears.

"What about that one?" the man said, nodding toward Henry.

Mavis looked at Rose and Rose looked at Mavis and they both looked at Mr. Duffy, who said, "That one's mine."

Bingo!

Their plan had worked!

Mr. Duffy had fallen in love with Henry.

Rose and Mavis slapped and snapped and fist-bumped.

At the end of the day, Miss Jeeter drove Rose back to Magnolia Estates with that plastic flower flapping in the breeze. When they got to the gate and the new gatekeeper slid the little window open, Miss Jeeter said, "Luanne Jeeter here to see Cora Tully." Then she turned and winked at Rose.

When they drove by the Simms' house, Amanda was sitting on her porch with some other girls. Rose felt confidence float in through the open car window and settle on her shoulders. Here she was, Rose Tully, sitting beside her best friend, not worrying one bit about those girls.

She waved at them.

Amanda waved back.

Some of the other girls waved, as well.

When Miss Jeeter turned into the Tullys' winding driveway, she honked the horn at Monroe Tucker, who was trimming the azaleas. Then she waved to Mrs. Tully and some ladies drinking tea on the screened porch. Rose and Mavis leaned out the window of the car and hollered, "Yoo-hoo!" Then they collapsed on the back seat, giggling hysterically.

When Miss Jeeter stopped the car in front of Pete and Larry, Rose said goodbye and dashed upstairs to her bedroom.

She sat on the canopy bed and thought about the very first day that Mavis had been here, inspecting Rose's things and saying "holy cannoli."

She remembered how she had been worried that Mavis might think having a doll bed in her room was babyish, but Mavis hadn't.

Then Rose walked over to the dresser and looked at herself in the mirror.

The Rose looking back at her was a different Rose from the one who had been here that day.

Rose smiled and whispered hello to this new Rose.

The brave Rose who didn't have that tornado of worry spinning around her nearly every minute of the day.

The Rose who had a best friend.

The Rose who went to Wonderland with Mavis.

ACKNOWLEDGMENTS

With heartfelt thanks:

To my editor, Janine O'Malley, for loving Rose and Mavis from the get-go;

To the rest of my FSG team, for their hard work and much-appreciated contributions: Melissa Warten, Aimee Fleck, Jen Bricking, Jennifer Sale, Melissa Zar, and Kelsey Marrujo;

To my agent, Barbara Markowitz, and her husband, Harvey, for everything;

To Michele Kophs, my event coordinator, for keeping me organized and sane;

To my husband, Willy, for never complaining about eating leftovers;

To my son, Grady, just because;

To my Asheville writers group, The Secret Gardeners, for being kindred spirits and dear friends;

To my sister, Linda, for traveling this rocky road of life with me;

To my niece, mean ole Amanda Simm, for being my Asheville family;

To Monika Schroeder, for being my grumpy companion in the balcony;

And to all the parents, teachers, and librarians who connect young readers with books.

It really does take a village.

Thank you all.

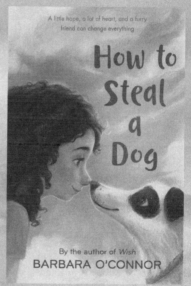